GOING
SOLO

TARA MILLS

Going Solo

ISBN: 978-0-9903084-5-4
Copyright © 2015, Tara Mills
Cover Art by Steven Novak

This book is a work of fiction and any resemblance to persons, living or dead, or places, events or locales is purely coincidental. The characters are products of the author's imagination and used fictitiously.

Published in the United States of America by Sherman Hills Press.

Sherman Hills Press

Stories with a heartbeat.

Dedicated to my many music teachers,
both band and choir.

And for my husband, who can make even *my* voice
sound beautiful when we harmonize together.
You're awesome.

I'd also like to give a big thank you to my fabulous
beta readers: Leigh Lee, Nola Cross, Lynn Muhich,
Mark Morris, and, of course, my wonderful
husband. I also want to thank Steven Novak for
another fantastic cover.

Where would I be without you?

Chapter One

Shasta Kovich stood in the quiet hallway, eighteen floors up, glaring at the once elegant flocked and foiled wallpaper, growing more furious by the minute. For ten of those minutes she'd been alternately pressing the doorbell and knocking—without any answer. Now she was on the verge of blowing the top right off her pressure cooker.

She scowled at the art deco sconce on the wall and muttered, "Five more seconds and I'm out of here. This is bullshit."

"One, two," she counted. A door farther down the hallway opened and a man's dark head poked out.

Hel-lo.

Then he frowned at her. "Shasta?"

Shit. Was she at the wrong door?

"Yes?"

He scanned her from head to toe and his face twitched in unmistakable distaste. *What the hell?* Gorgeous did not mean he was automatically excused for something like that. She shifted on her spiked boots and glared back. It was blatantly apparent he didn't like what he saw.

Who does he think he is, anyway?

Giving her a curt nod, he beckoned her over.

"You're late. And you're at the wrong door. That's my private apartment. *This* is the studio. I thought Sarah told you all this."

Shasta would have stomped her way over if her feet didn't hurt so damn bad. What a prick. Nobody lectures her. Simmering, she scowled back at him. "Must have been lost in translation."

He stepped aside to let her in. The enclosed studio was dead ahead. Looking through the large window she saw an upright piano, music stand, and a couple of chairs. Acoustic tiles covered the walls and ceiling.

"You can hang your coat there." He pointed to the small closet on her right then went into the studio and took a seat at the piano.

Shasta slipped out of her black leather jacket and hung it up. He swiveled on the bench when she walked in.

"Shut the door."

"Nice to meet you, too." *Asshole.* "Ever use the word *please*?"

This guy's manners sucked.

Blake Adams ignored the scathing question. "Have you been practicing?"

She shifted her shoulders, easily shoved off her confident footing once again. "A little."

That earned an even deeper frown. "Let's hope you haven't ruined your recovery."

Shasta's jaw dropped. The gall! *"What?"*

"You heard me. You had vocal cord surgery. You were supposed to be on total voice rest until you came to see me. I don't want you singing anywhere *but* here until I'm confident you know what you're doing. And keep unnecessary chit-chat to a minimum, even whispers. If you have to gab with your friends, do it on-line or text them instead. Use your thumbs and give your voice a break."

Shasta was roasting in her gravy now. "Listen up. I have a number one hit. I know what I'm doing."

"Correction. You *had* a number one hit. It's already dropped to fourteen, and your concert tour was cut short when you blew out your voice *because*—" The jerk drew out the word longer than necessary. "You Don't Know Dick about singing."

When all she could do was sputter, he bludgeoned on. "I listened to your CD and," he grimaced, "it was painful, but here's the thing—the music itself wasn't bad. You have raw talent. Notice, I'm emphasizing *raw* for a reason. You might even have a future in music *if* you listen and apply yourself. Otherwise, you'll just be another in the long line of one-hit-wonders."

If she had laser beams for eyes and could burn him where he sat, he'd be charred and smoking right now. "I don't like you very much."

Nothing. Not even a raised eyebrow from him. "Your feelings for me are irrelevant. All I want to know is will you listen and follow my direction?"

She could feel the hostility sweating out of her pores and seriously wondered if she *could* buckle under for him at this point. After a lengthy stare down, she finally grumbled, "Do I have a choice?"

"Not if you want to hang onto your record contract."

"Fine." She was not happy about this. There had to be someone she could complain to. Her agent, Sarah, was definitely going to get an earful.

"Let's get started. Why don't you run through your typical warm-up for me? How do you prepare your voice?"

He'd stumped her. "What?"

"Show me your pre-flight check." He threw up his hand, waiting. His instructions weren't getting through. A foreign language would have been just as helpful.

"Oh no, you've gotta be kidding me." The look of dawning horror on his face wasn't reassuring.

"I don't know what you're talking about." She flapped her arms, beyond befuddled.

To her amazement, he gripped his forehead and groaned. His eyes tightly shut, he muttered under his breath, his body gently rocking on the piano bench.

"Hey!" Her hand went to her hip and she

scowled at him, outwardly pissed though her heart was knocking like an oil-starved engine. "What the hell is your problem?"

He dropped his hand and looked at her as if she'd just ruined his life. "Have you ever had a voice lesson?"

She hesitated on the answer, though he obviously knew it. "No."

It was a strange thing to watch a classy guy like this almost lose it. There was a heavy sigh. He dropped his head and bit his lower lip. The letter f was already on its way out of his mouth when he stopped short of saying the rest of the four letter word. Why not just say the fucking word?

Back in command of himself, Adams studied her for a quiet moment, no doubt formulating his plan of attack. Finally, he asked, "Do you ever stretch beforehand? You know, loosen up your body, your shoulders, neck, anything?"

She frowned. Was he for real? "No."

"How about deep breathing?" The smidgen of hope she saw in his face didn't stand a chance.

"No," she persisted, even more concerned about his quackery. What did all this have to do with singing?

"Do you know the difference between a head voice and a chest voice?"

"What the fuck?"

"Please don't use that language here."

"Fine."

"Take a minute to stretch up, hands in the air. Breathe in then slowly let it out."

"Are you serious?"

"Shasta, this is important."

Though she felt stupid and not entirely on-board with his approach to voice training, she did what he asked. She shifted her shoulders. She rolled her head and loosened her neck. She shook out her arms and opened her chest. Her yawn was accidental and spontaneous but it seemed to excite him. He had her yawn a few more times to open her throat and notice how it felt through her torso.

Then he had her hum. She was absolutely calling Sarah as soon as she got out of here. This guy was nuts.

"Are you relaxed?" he asked.

"As much as I can be." The whole experience felt weird, and she wasn't comfortable doing all this bullshit in front of a total stranger.

"Good." He spun on the bench and faced the piano. "Let's see what you've got." He hit a key and held it. "Give me a C, closed lips, hum it."

She mimicked the note and he looked up sharply. "You're flat. Try again."

She took another breath and repeated herself. His frown darkened.

"Don't you have *any* ear at all? Listen to this." He stabbed the key repeatedly, making her jerk with every irritating strike.

"Again!" He hit the key and finally she satisfied him—briefly. "Hold it as long as you can. Again."

Shasta sang the single note, but it faded out before the piano went silent.

"That's what I thought," he muttered and spun to face her, straddling the bench. "You need to decide whether you want to be a rock star or a musician, because you can't be both."

"What do you mean?"

"Choose—performer or musician."

"They're the same."

"No." His head dropped slightly to one side as he peered at her. "A *performer* is an entertainer, conscious of their image. It's about the dancing and theatrics as much as it is the music. They have no problem kicking over their equipment and trashing instruments during a show. A *musician* not only has a deep love of music itself, but a respect for the tools of the craft. So far you've been a performer, utterly abusing your instrument—your voice. A true musician wouldn't lay their guitar down on its strings. That's basically what you've been doing."

His dark eyes bored into her and she looked away. "I want to be a musician," she mumbled, aware of the distinctions.

"Good. Let's see if we can turn you into one. First things first, open your pants."

"I don't fucking think so!" She backed away.

With a snort of derision, he stood and walked toward her. "Relax, you're not my type and this isn't remotely sexual."

He moved behind her and stood there. Tense and paranoid, she looked over her shoulder at him. His patience was clearly wearing thin because he snapped, "Open those ridiculous leather pants you've poured yourself into or I will."

Horrified at the thought, Shasta undid the fly and just about jumped out of her stiletto boots when his hand came around from behind and settled over her abdomen. She felt his jolt of surprise at her navel piercing under his palm. He surprised her right back by giving the tiny sterling silver eighth note a little flick. He stopped it from swinging a second later with the press of his hand.

Frozen with shock and wariness, she inhaled sharply when he leaned close to her ear and said, "Breathe."

She'd never been so conscious of breathing...or of a man's touch.

He heaved a sigh of displeasure. "Wrong."

"How can I *breathe* wrong? I've been doing it my entire life." She was just as exasperated as he sounded.

"You are. You're paying too much attention to keeping your stomach flat. Put your hand where mine is."

She placed her hand over her stomach and he covered it with his. A simple, unexpected touch and now her heart was racing. It pissed her off.

"Breathe," he said softly. "In through the nose, out through the mouth."

She inhaled, then exhaled, but didn't notice anything unusual. "Yeah, so?"

"Wrong. All wrong. Inhale." She drew in a breath and he said sharply. "I said *inhale.* Our hands aren't moving, notice that?"

"My lungs are higher."

"Your diaphragm is here and you're only using a fraction of your lung capacity." He pressed into her abdomen and literally shoved the air out of her. Thank god she didn't fart, too.

"Stand up tall and bring the air down lower. Full complete breaths. Relax. Your shoulders shouldn't move up and down."

She tried again.

"Better. Keep going." He stepped around her and quietly watched for a few minutes.

"Why am I doing this?" Shasta felt ridiculous, not to mention a little light headed.

"Because a person who doesn't know how to breathe isn't going to be able to sing. I want long, sustained, strong notes coming from you and that isn't going to happen until you learn how to breathe properly. You have an assignment. Every night when you go to bed, I want you to hold your abdomen and focus on how you're breathing until it becomes so natural you don't have to think about it anymore. In the meantime, keep your hand on your diaphragm as a reminder."

He sat down at the piano and hit the C again. "Sing."

She sang, clear and strong and he turned and nodded. "Good, keep it going. Hold it as long as you can without straining."

As the note faded away he finally smiled for the first time. She almost cried with gratitude.

"Much better."

She hated how much his approval meant to her already.

"You can close your pants now," he said a hint of amusement. "When are you coming again?"

"Thursday." She turned away with a blush and zipped her fly.

"Wear something comfortable next time. Something you can actually breathe in—and that includes shoes." He glanced at her sexy leather boots. "The last thing I want you thinking about here is your Goth image, got it?"

"Goth image?" She snorted then caught the

hard look in his eye. He was serious. Wrong, but serious. "Fine."

Shasta walked out of the sound room feeling ignorant and diminished. Glaring through the glass at the new bane of her existence, she saw him turn back to the keys. His long graceful fingers caressed a sultry jazz number out of the vibrating strings of his piano as she closed the outer door behind her.

♫

Bose dipped her eggroll in the puddle of duck sauce on the edge of her plate. She shook her head before taking the next bite. "Well that sucks. How were you supposed to know he *lived* there too?"

Shasta threw up her hand and grumbled, "I know, right?"

"So are you going to quit sulking and tell me how it went?"

Shasta gave her friend a noncommittal shrug while swirling her fork through the rice and vegetable dish in front of her. "Hard to say. All he did was lecture me and talk about breathing. I suppose the guy knows what he's talking about. I mean, they wouldn't force me to see him if he didn't. But he's such a *dick*."

Bose frowned and swept her wispy, brown bangs out of her eyes with the back of her hand. "Example?"

Shasta set her fork down and reached for her water. "For starters, he made that bad odor face when he saw me for the first time. You know the one. Like something nasty crawled up his nostrils and died. I gotta tell ya, I was a little insulted."

"No shit! What an ass. I hope you told him off."

"I was about to, but then he started dissing our music next."

Now Bose was offended. "Hell no! Unbelievable." She stabbed a baby carrot so hard the tines of her fork make an unpleasant *screech* on the plate.

"He's just so unbelievably rude," Shasta continued. "It's his tone of voice, the way he talked to me—*at* me. The guy thinks he's hot shit. I could totally tell. You wouldn't believe how tempted I was to slam his fingers in the piano or pick up the music stand and bash him over the head with it."

Bose sputtered on a laugh. "Well I heard he's not the only one who thinks he's pretty hot."

"No way." Shasta's disbelief was an act. Blake Adams had set her radar pinging before the first sneer. Her attraction cooled dramatically after that.

"Way. Dee told me he's gorgeous." Bose watched her closely, waiting for a confirmation or denial.

Shasta set her water down and gave a grudging shrug. "She would. Dee likes those arrogant types. I suppose he qualifies." Taking up her fork, she was about to poke a pea pod when she paused to ask a question. "How would Dee know anyway?"

"Remember when she was going out with that guy from Pyramid Records?"

"What was his name again?" asked Shasta.

"No idea. Doesn't matter. Anyway he took her to one of those swanky functions, black tie and all that shit, and she actually met him there."

"Him who?"

"Blake Adams, that's who. And do you know who he was with?"

"Why would I care?" Damn it, now she *was* curious.

"Valerie Walters."

"Shut up!" This time, Shasta's disbelief was real.

Her reaction excited Bose. "I'm serious."

It couldn't be true. Could it?

"What would the darling of Broadway be doing with a virtual nobody?" asked Shasta.

Bose wagged her fork at Shasta. "I don't think he's as unknown as you think he is."

"Huh." Shasta sat back and pondered this little nugget of information.

♫

Hours later, Blake escaped his bedroom, softly

closing the door behind him. Only then did he reach for the switch on the wall. A brass lamp with jade accents at the far side of the living room blazed on, the glossy sheen of the dark cherry cabinet beneath it suffused with an amber glow. Going over to the recessed bar, he poured himself two fingers of brandy, turning the exquisite crystal in his hand to admire the rich color before raising it to his lips. An explosion of spiced fruit and fig filled his head, the heat coating his tongue and infiltrating his sinuses. He held it there, savoring the moment before swallowing. The warmth spread through him from the inside out.

Crossing to one of the large windows, he looked out over the city. Lights glittered against the black velvet night. It was one a.m. and like so many other nights, he was up, driven to his piano to tinker with the notes that kept him from dropping off to sleep.

He turned and set the glass on top of the instrument then took a seat at the black baby grand and closed his eyes. His fingers found the keys and he brushed across them ever so lightly, already feeling the hum in his chest before he even drew a single note.

It would begin with an F. Eyes closed, head cocked to one side he pressed the key and smiled faintly when it answered the intoxicating note in his head.

He played for over an hour, alive to the need to create music out of thin air.

The bedroom door eventually opened and his beautiful overnight guest wandered out and leaned against the jamb wearing his discarded shirt, seductively unbuttoned. She was stunning without even trying, but she liked to play the game anyway, knowing exactly how to pose for maximum effect. The corner of his mouth twitched when she slowly tousled her fiery red hair and pouted at him.

"Come back to bed," she beckoned softly.

"In a few minutes." Closing his eyes once more, he continued to play, dismissing her from his mind as he gave himself up to the music flowing through him.

♫

Upset, but not surprised, Valerie glared at the hulking black instrument, her only rival for Blake's attention. Returning to his dark bedroom alone, she fumed, knowing how it would go. She'd wait until the wee hours of the morning, her hopes for one more round of lovemaking unfulfilled. When he was immersed in his own head like this, she doubted he even remembered she was there.

Why did she put up with it? She didn't know.

No, that wasn't true. She knew all right. When

he focused on her with the same intensity as he did that damn piano, he made her body sing, sent her flying to the heavens, and held her there like a suspended note until she vibrated back to earth, weak and dizzy. Sometimes her radiant glow could last for an hour or more afterwards. She'd learned to schedule her photo shoots after spending the night with Blake because he was better than any cosmetic at bringing her cool beauty to life.

With a wiggle of her shoulders, she dropped his shirt to the floor where she'd found it and slid back into bed. Disappointed, yet resigned, she turned on her side and hugged his pillow to her face, inhaling the lingering scent of him and the cologne he favored.

Swaddled in irritation, Val cursed herself for her weakness. She cursed Blake for his indifference.

Chapter Two

Shasta tossed and turned in her bed, brooding over the session she'd had with Blake Adams earlier that day. He'd made her feel inadequate, inferior...insignificant. Those feelings were painfully familiar. She'd grown up with them. Never again.

She'd managed to get through to her agent, Sarah, by the time she'd hit the sidewalk outside his building, but the effort had been pointless. Oh sure, Sarah apologized up and down for how he'd treated her, but the decision was made and there was no renegotiating this one. Shit.

Flinging her arm out to the side, Shasta struck the pillow next to her with the back of her hand. Did it make her feel any better? Not really. She squeezed her eyes closed and focused on calming the bitchy rant in her head. Only then did she notice how she was breathing.

The rebel in her wanted to wipe Blake's directive from her mind, but that was impossible. She slowly slipped her hand down her ribs and inched the bottom of her tank up until she felt warm skin. Covering her right hand with her left, just as he'd done, she focused on breathing. Her hands rose and fell as her abdomen expanded with air.

Unbidden, the memory of his large hand pressed firmly against her rushed back. She didn't want to remember the spread of those fingers—but she did. She wished she could have seen his face when he discovered her piercing. On second thought, maybe not. He was too straight-laced to appreciate piercings and tattoos. If he could manage to keep future comments to himself, she wouldn't have any reason to mention the stick up his ass.

She ventured farther down, wondering exactly how much he might have felt. Had he brushed up against the top of her panties or did he stop just shy of the elastic? With those outrageously long pianists' fingers of his, it wouldn't surprise her if he made panty contact. Imagining it made her heart skip a beat.

Hang on, *why* was she wasting a single second wondering about all this? It shouldn't matter to her. Blake Adams was cool, aloof, and dripping with the kind of contempt that only came from being born to comfort and privilege. No doubt a guy like him wouldn't see the point in being polite and considerate to anyone outside his cushy socio-economic stratum.

Screw that! Just because they come from different backgrounds doesn't give him the right to treat her like crap. She mattered, damn it! It was insulting the way the arrogant son of a bitch sized her up and wrote her off in seconds. But he was wrong about her, so wrong, and she was going to prove it.

Shasta took a deep breath; aware she'd worked herself into a spiky mood again. Refocusing her mind, she visualized calm scenes. She was the queen of serene. Maybe not. Shifting gears, she pictured the periwinkle blue walls of her compact kitchen. As her breathing slowed back to a more relaxed rhythm, Blake's handsome face emerged from the blue background and fired her up again.

Ugh! What did it take to banish the bastard from her brain? Nothing was working. To her growing disgust, she imagined him strutting around with Valerie Walters on his arm. The internet was probably full of photos of those two. She grudgingly conceded they'd make an attractive pair. So what? *Let it go, Shasta*. Good advice. One minute, two minutes. Damn it! She knew already she'd be looking them up on Google in the morning.

♫

Bright sunshine illuminated the front quarter of Blake's apartment, bathing everything near the windows in a golden glow. As the sun rose, it nudged the line of light across the floor, over furnishings, and up the opposite wall. The heat felt good, warming him in his dark gray, v-neck pullover as he sat working at the piano. He'd been at it for hours, marking up the blank staffs printed on the sheets of paper in front of him, absorbed by the insistent tune in his head.

He paused and frowned at what he just wrote. Shifting the pencil to his left hand, he played the notes, humming along in his mellow baritone.

"No," he said to the empty room, a habit of his when he was working something out.

He tried a variation on what was written and preferred that. Blake backtracked and tapped out a string of notes, making minor changes before picking up his pencil and marking them down. Now he needed to hear all of this in one go.

He stuck the pencil between his teeth and it stretched the corners of his mouth on either side. Unconcerned, he flipped the sheets of music back to the beginning to take another run at it. He could hardly contain his excitement as he followed the music, his fingers caressing the keys. His head bobbed in time, his foot tapped beneath him, and his heart soared when he reached the end. Blake tugged the pencil out of his mouth and broke into a big smile that withered when he noticed the clock on the mantle.

"Shit! Is that the time?"

He leaped up and checked his watch. The timepieces agreed. He muttered another curse and left the pages in disarray. They'd be there when he got back.

Blake ran for the front closet, grabbed his long, black overcoat, and thrust his arms through the sleeves. He grabbed his keys off the side table on his way out. There wasn't much he could do about his faded jeans and casual shirt.

Oh well. She'd forgiven him for a lot worse.

♫

Shasta sat at her little kitchen table, facing the window, her laptop open in front of her. A mug of cold coffee sat on her right. A plate with dried yolk and the crusty remains of her toast sat ignored on her left. She'd been on the computer for so long the plate was going to need to soak. With her left heel pulled flush against her bottom, her chin resting on her knee, she scrolled over candid images of Blake Adams and Valerie Walters, one after another. It was almost as bad as typing in John F. Kennedy Jr. *Shit*. Those two were gorgeous, all decked out for this opening night, that benefit, and other assorted fashion-fests. She didn't honestly believe there'd be so many to go through when she silently amused herself last night with the idea of looking them up.

To see that woman dripping off his arm like jewels, draped over his shoulder like a flaming, fox stole, gave Shasta a sour stomach. She actually clenched her teeth at how Mr. I'm-Too-Sexy-For-This-World was shown pulling Valerie by the hand away from her fans and photographers on their way into yet another exclusive event requiring formalwear. The man looked freaking incredible in a tux. The bitch never looked bad, either. Damn.

Okay, maybe calling Valerie Walters a bitch was a little over the top. Shasta had no way of knowing what she was like as a person. Then again, exquisite on the outside didn't necessarily mean exquisite on the inside. Just look at the a-hole holding her hand. Case in point.

What was the purpose of looking all this up anyway? She tried to remember. Oh yeah, to prove to herself Blake Adams was nothing special and had better treat her with more respect from now on.

Shasta snorted at herself. Yeah, well, that backfired. She and Adams weren't merely from different backgrounds and parts of the city—they were in entirely different orbits.

She knew a hell of a lot more about him now. For starters, Blake's father, Simon, was a world famous conductor. For the last four years, he'd been director of the Royal Vienna Symphony Orchestra. Blake's mom, Louisa, besides coming from pedigreed American stock with Mayflower roots, was a distinguished cellist, and important in her own right. Judging by the pictures Shasta turned up earlier that morning, Blake had inherited his father's dark, good looks and his mother's refinement and poise. His talent came from both.

She groaned just recalling his biography. The guy had a freaking biography—*on the web*! Prep school background, classical training from Juilliard, and then he did an about-face and pursued jazz and contemporary music after that. Not only was he in demand as a studio musician, with credit on dozens of albums and CD's, but he was an emerging composer. Why the hell was a guy like that giving her voice training? It made no sense.

She actually squirmed when she remembered pompously pulling the ol' *I have a number one hit* on him. Ugh. How embarrassing. No wonder he wasn't impressed. The worst thing is, she knew jazz—the old stuff anyway. She loved it. She just didn't keep up with the current performers. Oh sure, she was familiar with the biggest front men, everyone was, even people who didn't follow jazz would recognize a few names, but the rest, she was clueless.

To her dismay, the resentful daughter of a sleazy lounge singer sensed her own inferiority all over again. She hadn't felt this...inconsequential in years. *What if you really* can't *leave your crappy roots behind?* She'd looked after herself for nine years. Eighteen months ago, *Velvet Bitches* hit it big. Now, when she finally felt on solid ground, Shasta felt the specter of her past lurching up behind her in a stale cloud of smoke, wearing cheap heels, a shiny polyester dress, and belting it out there in a slurred, gravelly voice. Just the thought of her negligent mother made Shasta want to recoil. If only she could lock the woman away somewhere before she resurfaced and embarrassed her again. How long before Cokie Kovich turned up looking for money? If she ever got wind of Shasta's short-lived success, she'd track her down like a bloodhound.

Maybe she should move again. Make it harder to find her. Seriously considering it, Shasta got up and dumped the last of her tepid coffee down the drain then set her plate in the sink and ran water over it. Her stomach didn't feel so good anymore.

♫

Blake bounded off the subway and took the steps two at a time up to ground level. He held the bouquet of mixed flowers close to his chest, protecting it from getting crushed as he cut around the other pedestrians.

Sprinting half a block, he caught hold of the wrought iron railing at the bottom of the staircase and it propelled him into a hard right turn and up the stone steps. He was panting for air when he pressed the call button. She buzzed him inside without a word and he ran for the elevator, the slap of his shoes echoing on the tiles. The ride up allowed him to catch his breath. He straightened his jacket and blindly finger combed his hair, doing his best to tidy himself. He was released at the fourth floor. The door opened down the hallway before he reached it. It was one of the best sounds.

That old familiar sense of coming home swept over him and Blake felt his body finally begin to relax. Smiling now, he checked his stride, eyeing the flowers for any damage before he hid them behind his back.

Then he saw her and his smile grew even wider. He'd never loved anyone more.

"You look beautiful."

Chapter Three

The delicate old woman leaned into his warm hug and accepted her kiss on the forehead. Her pretty cornflower blue eyes sparkled up at him. "You cut it kind of close."

"I'm here, Clara, on time." Blake laughed and stepped inside so she could shut the door. Then he presented the bouquet with a flourish. "Sorry, I didn't like what they had for roses today."

"Oh, honey, stop spoiling me. You don't have to bring flowers every time you visit."

"Hush." He caressed her cheek, loving her so much. "I know I don't *have* to. But I *like* to."

She ran her fingers over the petals then took a deep sniff and sighed. "I still remember the first flowers you brought me."

He chuckled. "Do you? What were they?"

"Daisies. You were nine."

He shook his head, amazed at how vivid the memory was now that she'd reminded him. "That's right. I seem to remember a card too."

She reached up and brushed the backs of her fingers along the underside of his chin, a tender look in her eye. "You made it yourself."

He did. He'd stayed in during recess and used

31

red construction paper, carefully cutting around a picture of the two of them. Clara was hugging him from behind, peeking over his head as they both smiled for the camera. He'd glued that photo to the front, the white doily behind it serving as a frilly frame. He wrote his message inside.

They looked at each other now, neither mentioning what he wrote, but both clearly recalling his boyhood wish she could be his real mother, rather than just his nanny.

"You were, you know," he told her softly, unable to keep from smiling just as tenderly back at her. "Are you sorry all you had was me?"

"I couldn't have loved my own children more. You were my little boy."

"Still am. Are you all set for lunch?"

"I should put these in water first."

"I'll get the vase down for you." Blake cut around her and entered the cozy little apartment. Going into the dated kitchen, he went right for an upper cabinet, drawing out her favorite crystal vase, the one he gave her as a birthday present long ago.

He turned, showing her which he chose. "Will this do?"

She laughed and a look of affection passed between them. "Perfect."

As always, Blake gave Clara his arm on their

walk to the coffee shop at the end of the street. Neither acknowledged how his courtly gesture had become a necessary one. She leaned on him more, needing his steady support. Nor did they mention how their pace had gradually slowed over the years. He merely checked his stride and made it appear as if they were simply taking a leisurely stroll. Blake did all he could to preserve his beloved nanny's dignity. He knew she understood. She had a habit of looking up at him with a gentle smile and patting his arm. Her silent thank you was enough for him.

"Are you ever going to introduce me to your lady friend?" Clara asked after they ordered their sandwiches.

Blake stirred his coffee then set the spoon in the saucer before picking up the plain white cup. "No."

"It's been at least a year. She's a lovely woman. You look nice together."

He coughed in mid swallow and had to yank a napkin from the dispenser on the table. Mopping up the droplets of coffee in front of him, he shook his head, unable to meet her gaze. "It isn't...we aren't...*like* that." Wadding the damp paper, he set it aside and looked up with a bleak expression.

She frowned with concern. "All this time and it's not a relationship?"

"I know it must sound crazy to you. It's complicated." And simple. Sometimes the buddy system, with occasional sex, was all you need.

"You don't love her." It was a clarification, not a question.

He could feel his cheek twitch before he snorted, unable to deny it. "No." He dropped heavily against the backrest of his chair and sighed. "I don't know what I'm still doing there. We don't have a future." He shook his head again, just picturing how awful it would be. "The last thing I want to do is give another kid parents like mine."

Her reaction to his confession was instantaneous. "You want a child?"

"Eventually." He gave Clara a cockeyed smile and picked up his cup again. "Two," he added.

"Really?"

She was breathtaking when she smiled like that. It took years off her beloved face, at least in *his* eyes.

He winked at her. "Don't look so surprised. I hated being an only child. I want two kids, close together. It doesn't even matter what sex. I just don't want either of them to ever feel that alone."

Clara reached across the table and they gripped hands. He was careful not to squeeze too tight. Her hands felt alarmingly delicate these days. Her skin was so thin and transparent the blue veins rose right out of the top. He skimmed his thumb over one, thinking it was still the loveliest hand he'd ever held, age spots and all.

♫

As the floors blinked by above the elevator door, Shasta looked down at herself one more time. She was disgusted at how much time and thought she'd put into coming up with an acceptable wardrobe for her stupid voice lesson and yet, she'd agonized over it anyway.

The light for the eighteenth floor lit up with a pleasant musical *ding* and the door slid back. This time she went to the right door and knocked—and knocked. She was just raising her hand to knock again when the door opened.

Shasta swallowed—hard. Her hand hung suspended in mid-rap as she stared at the man in front of her. He grinned, his startlingly white smile brilliant against the warm chocolate luster of his face.

"Blake, I think it's for you," he called over his shoulder. Then he slipped around her carrying an instrument case. "Later."

Shasta turned and stared after him as he stepped onto the elevator she'd just exited.

"Hey," Blake called to her. "Aren't you coming

in?"

"Hm?"

"Get in here."

Closing the door carefully, she turned on Blake with wide, star-struck eyes and whispered, "That was Damien Morris."

"Mmm hmm. You know, you don't have to knock on the studio door if you're expected. Just come in. It's not locked." He peered at her more closely. "Did you hear what I said?"

Still dizzy with disbelief, her gaze cut back to him. "You're working with Damien Morris?"

He snickered at that. "No, we were just jamming a bit."

Now *she* laughed. "You. *You* were jamming with Damien Morris?"

"It happens. Get in here. The clock is ticking." Walking away, he waved her into the studio, presuming she'd follow. He was right.

Blake settled onto the bench and turned to give Shasta a cursory once-over. "What are you wearing?"

She bristled, her hands on her hips. "My yoga outfit. You got a problem with it?"

The ass looked amused. "Nope. It'll work."

He sat there, simply waiting for her. She stared right back, waiting too. Finally, he gave an exas–

perated sigh. "Where is your hand supposed to be?"

"Oh." She laughed at herself, finally understanding what he expected from her.

Blake frowned. "Are you breathing?"

"Yes." Another hiss. She was getting good at those.

"Could have fooled me. I see your bra size is growing, but your hand hasn't moved. Stand up, straight and tall, and try again."

She discovered it wasn't easy to take a deep, calming breath while annoyed. It took her three tries.

"There it is." To her surprise, he actually smiled. "What did you do just there?"

"Besides refrain from beating you senseless?" She had no control over her sass either. Damn.

His left eyebrow took a comical leap. "Obviously."

"I relaxed."

"No, you took a full breath." When she just looked at him, he nodded. "See, you *do* know how. Show me again."

For five minutes that's all he had her work on; breathe in, breathe out. The guy would make one hell of a yoga instructor.

He spun on the bench and raised his hands over the keys. "On the exhale." He hit middle C—a key that was seriously beginning to irritate her.

Shasta nailed the damn note.

"Excellent. Did you hear that?"

She rolled her eyes. "Of course."

"Then what am I talking about?"

"Umm...the *note*?"

"No—well yes, the note, but why am I asking?"

Shasta shrugged. "Beat's me."

"You hit it the first time. Why weren't you flat?"

"Because I'm breathing right?"

"Exactly."

She snapped her fingers, feeling sassy all of a sudden. "Piece of cake."

They moved on to scales next and he listened carefully to every note she hit. When Blake finally turned from the piano, Shasta was floating on a luxurious cushion of cockiness until ol' sourpuss brought up her music again.

He studied her thoughtfully. "So you *can* sing."

She gave him a frosty glare. "Nice. I *do* have a record out."

"That wasn't singing." Her jaw was back to swinging by its hinges. *What a jerk*! "Go home and listen to it," he continued before she could mouth off. "What you did here today is singing. What you did on that album was nothing more than vocal butchery with a little screaming thrown in. There's a difference and it's the reason you damaged your voice. You may have been a novelty act, but you've shown me you can be more. Find your voice, Shasta. It's in there, and it's beautiful. Nice alto."

Five minutes later—feeling oddly conflicted—Shasta jabbed the ground floor button in the elevator. She loathed the man, yet couldn't stop herself from floating on the buzz his encouraging compliments gave her. It was as if there was nothing more precious in the world. Fans would swarm her for autographs whenever they recognized her. Why didn't that kind of attention give her the same heady rush *his* approval did? She was seriously twisted.

♫

Back at her modest little apartment later that evening, Shasta put on her *Velvet Bitches* CD and finally gave it an objective listen. It wasn't pleasant. The gritty, grungy sound she'd worked so hard to cultivate made her wince in pain now that she understood what Blake Adams was talking about. No wonder she'd needed surgery and complete vocal rest afterwards.

She padded into the bathroom and looked at herself in the mirror, long and hard, then washed off her heavy makeup. The dramatic sweep of eyeliner she'd applied that morning took a little extra work, but when she was finished, her skin glowed like a pink, little baby's.

Shasta actually liked her face. To her relief, she didn't see much of her mother there, beyond bone structure. She'd spent countless hours over the years, wondering about her nameless father. In truth, she didn't think of him as anything more than an opportunistic sperm donor, but she had to thank him for her deep, brown eyes and almond skin. Her pert little nose must have come from him as well. Cokie's was sharper, like a sail turned sideways. Her mother's eyes were smaller and set deeper in the sockets, unlike Shasta's. She had large, expressive eyes. Even their lashes were different.

Tugging on the fading pink ends of her hair, she made a face. Her lighter roots were growing out from underneath too. Should she dye it all dark again or let the natural light brown come back? She snorted at her reflection. Maybe Blake was right. What if she *was* a novelty act, more conscious of her image than her ability?

Bullshit. That was bullshit. What was wrong with her tonight?

Shasta yanked her shirt off over her head, taking her modest A-cups with it. Stepping over to the tub, she drew back the shower curtain and turned on the faucet. She needed to wash that man right out of her hair. She chuckled at the visual. Just like Mitzi Gaynor. That was the song she hummed as she stepped under the hot spray. It might just be time to pull out that old South Pacific album.

Her plan was forgotten by the time she returned to the living room carrying a virgin drink in a lowball glass. Shasta went searching through her music collection and found her Damien Morris CD instead. She put it on and flopped into her only comfy chair and let his soothing cornet lull her into a blissful stupor.

Slowly she opened her eyes and watched the glass of lemon-lime soda propped on her stomach gently rise and fall. Interesting. Without even realizing it, she was breathing properly. She laughed at the thought and almost spilled on herself.

That was when she set the glass aside and got up to flip through her old albums, finally pulling out Peggy Lee. She slid the record out of the cardboard jacket and turned it in the light, admiring its pristine condition. Frank had taken excellent care of his collection. She blew softly over the grooves then placed it on the turntable. Switching off the CD, she swayed to *Why Don't You Do Right?*

"Damn it, Frank. I told you I'd take care of you." Furious and despondent, she wiped her eyes and refused to cry. "Why couldn't you hold out a little longer?" Her voice broke anyway with her last helpless question. Sometimes she felt so desperately alone she ached inside.

These were Frank's records, his legacy, his only possessions. He'd left them to her. Why not? He didn't need them anymore, but she certainly did. Knowing all the old tunes by heart, Shasta sang along until her throat closed up, swollen by sorrow. All she could do was mouth the words. Her tears fell in earnest and she didn't try to stop them. Not this time. One after another, they made tracks down her clean face, ran under her jaw, slid along her neck, and seeped into the frayed collar of her favorite t-shirt. She was beyond caring. No one was here to see her lose it. Sometimes she just needed a good cry.

Frank was her mom's second husband, a sad, sweet drunk who fell for the wrong woman singing in his favorite bar. Cokie brought him home and dumped him on Shasta then hit the road again. Relieved of her parental responsibilities, her mom didn't make it back much after that.

The two dreamers bonded in a way Shasta never expected. She'd been on her own for so much of her childhood, slowly running through the cash her mom left in the cookie jar when she went away.

Shasta quickly learned how to economize so she wouldn't go hungry by the end of three weeks. It was the loneliness that really weighed her down. That is, until Frank got dumped with her. He looked just as shell-shocked by her mother's casual abandonment as she'd been at the age of thirteen. The only difference was, she'd been more resilient, determined—definitely more pissed off at her mom. Anger and attitude got her through the tough patches. Frank was too tender for that kind of treatment.

Shasta came to love the gentle man and he quietly returned the sentiment. Frank believed in her and was certain she was going to amount to something. He'd play his records and they'd lose themselves in the music, singing with Dinah Washington, Ella Fitzgerald, and Billy Holliday.

"Girl," he'd say with a proud gleam in his eye, "those pipes of yours are going to take you places. You could be the next Carmen McRae."

She'd loved him for that. His absolute confidence built her up from her knees...until she found herself back on them again, alone and damaged, her promising career already precariously perched on a precipice.

Now her hopes were pinned on another man—a man not nearly as sweet and charming as the first.

Where Frank boosted her confidence with encouragement, Blake tore her apart with his pointed criticisms. But it was impossible to argue when he was getting results. Maybe she needed the tough love. Frank recognized her ability, but he knew nothing about voice training. Though, to be fair, if either of them had understood what she needed, they couldn't have paid for it anyway.

She might not like Blake Adams, but she had a grudging respect for him. Maybe there was a little awe too—not that she'd ever tell him that. The guy's head was big enough. He didn't need the ego boost.

Only time would tell if he could rescue her sinking career.

Chapter Four

Shasta plucked the strings of her bass guitar, her chunky-heeled black boot tapping out the beat as Dee wailed on lead. Tipping her head sideways, she watched Bose doing her best with the vocals from behind the drums. She sounded terrible. Shasta chuckled to herself, wishing she could take over.

Dee's hand slipped off her steel strings and she turned to Bose, her irritation palpable. "You're rushing the beat again."

"Sue me." Bose shot back. "I've got too much shit in my head as it is. Just trying to remember the words and where I come in is fucking me up."

Dee took a deep breath and released it, her tight fingers splayed parallel with the floor. "Fine. I suppose *I* can sing it. I can't do any worse than you." She turned her glare on Shasta. "When are you going to be allowed to take over vocals again?"

Shasta squirmed on the inside. Her band-mates expected her back singing their old tunes, and the new ones they were presently working on, in the exact same way. That wasn't going to happen. The band, their sound, had to change if she was going to have a future in music. The irony was by singing the right way to preserve her voice there was a distinct possibility she was dooming the band. Once they saw their fans' reactions, her career might very well be over anyway. *Peachy*.

"Not sure. I'll keep you posted." She zipped her lip on the rest. No need to have them wig out on her now. Dee was already in one of her moods. "I haven't even begun to sing actual words with him yet. Adams's got me doing scales and shit. Singing long esses to see how long I can hold a note. He's a total freak about breath control."

Dee's lip curled and she gave a horrified shudder. "Scales? All you've been doing are scales so far? Unbelievable. He's hot an' all, but there's no way *I* could work with him. He's holding us up."

Shasta disagreed. He was helping her. She could already hear how much better she sounded after only two sessions. "Yeah, well. What can I do?"

"Not much." Bose gave the cymbal a little rap as she peered out from behind the drum set.

Shasta looked away, closing down the subject. It wasn't two beats later when Miri breezed in, unwinding a scarf from around her long, graceful neck. Catching how Dee's eyes narrowed on their keyboardist, Shasta started plucking out one of her favorite riffs, hoping to alleviate the tension.

Miri rolled back her stool and took a seat. She

set her soft leather shoulder bag on the floor where it collapsed in on itself.

Dee watched her silently then rolled her eyes at the other two before turning back to the latecomer. "Nice of you to join us."

Miri straightened her spine and gazed blandly back. "I told you I'd be late."

Dee shot a glance at the clock. "At this point, why bother coming in at all?"

A quiet hum sounded when Miri turned on the electric keyboard. "Quit ragging on me, bitch." She cracked her knuckles and played a few chords, arching her eyebrows at Dee.

Bose cleared her throat. "Ladies, ladies, take a Midol and leave the attitude at the door. Are we going to work or aren't we?"

Shasta snorted, brushing at the underside of her nose with the top of her hand. They all turned on her.

Dee's fist went to her hip. "What's so damn funny?"

Shasta couldn't have stopped her bout of chuckles if her life depended on it. "I've missed you guys."

Bose's right arm shot into the air, her drumstick raised, and a big grin on her face. "Hell yeah! It's good to have you back."

Miri smiled, her onyx eyes shining. "Missed you too, babe."

Dee wasn't quite so sweet. "See if you can hurry him along."

Shasta didn't care for Dee's tone or bossy attitude. "You do understand this is about healing and voice therapy, right? I can't exactly switch into an accelerated program for your convenience."

"Fine. At least learn the new lyrics. I want you ready to go as soon as you're cleared. I'm not singing lead on stage." She adjusted her wide shoulder strap and slid her hand down the neck of her guitar. "Hardcore Heaven, ladies. Count it off, Bose."

Shasta jumped in with her bass, incredibly pissed at how pushy Dee was getting. Now she was in the mood to set the bitch straight and tell her things were about to change. Only it would end up screwing Miri and Bose too. That wasn't something Shasta was prepared to do. Yet. Unfortunately, time was running out and she couldn't sit on this secret indefinitely.

♫

Shasta got to her lesson ten minutes early. She slipped inside and shrugged out of her leather jacket, stowing it, and her guitar, in the small closet.

A haunting melody took hold inside her. She slowly turned and saw Blake at the piano. His eyes were closed, his dark hair natural and untamed. It was miles beyond sexy. A stark contrast to the buttoned-up impression he usually made. Even his shirt looked softer today, the collar open and lying flat, as if his dry cleaners forgot the starch.

Her heartbeat galloped a little faster while she watched him play. She felt the music fill her in a register that was masculine to the core. Her body hummed, vibrated, along with the instrument. It spoke to her, pulled her toward him. She took careful, tentative steps, loath to disturb him—yet she couldn't deny the longing she felt to listen without a wall and window muffling the full, rich sound.

Poised at the small window in the door, she admired Blake's profile, his focus, the fluid dexterity of his fingers manipulating the keys. Her hand closed over the knob and she slowly turned it. His lashes swept up and he watched her sneak in. Shasta gave him a little smile and silently closed the door behind her. To her relief, he continued to the end of the song.

"That was beautiful," she said when he drew his hands back and flexed his fingers. "I know it from somewhere. I just can't place it."

He gave a little laugh. "Maybe this will help."

Blake played another, this one more rousing, and Shasta broke into a big smile. He shot one back at her, nodding his head as she shook hers.

She thought she knew now. "Peanuts, right?"

He touched the tip of his nose with his index finger. "Vince Guaraldi. This one's *Linus and Lucy*."

"What was the first?"

"*Christmastime is Here*."

"Ohh." She laughed at herself. The animated holiday scene came to her in vivid detail. "What else do you know?"

He veered into *Happy Birthday* with a cocky little grin.

Shasta burst out laughing. "Who would have thought *you* could have a playful side?"

He winked and slipped back into *Lucy and Linus* without missing a beat. "What are you wearing?"

"Pervert," she said, messing with him. He gave her a flat *give me a break* sort of look. Well, *she* thought it was funny. "My pregnancy jeans. There's a lot of stretch in the front panel."

His head tipped sideways and his eyebrow arched in surprise. His reaction made it impossible to keep a straight face. Snorting, she raised the bottom of her shirt, disproving the lie.

"Kidding, I'm kidding. They're low riders."

He nodded with the beat. "S*ooo* not pregnant."

"Definitely not. You have to have sex to get pregnant."

Now he was chuckling. Wrapping up the song, he sat back and took a deep breath, drawing out the exhale. "Ready for more scales?"

"That's all we've been doing. Can't we try something new today? You know, shake things up a bit?" Freaking scales again. He had no imagination.

"Actually, hang on." Blake rose from his bench and went out the opposite door. She heard a metal cabinet open. Peeking around the corner she saw him riffling through an open file drawer.

"Uh oh," she said under her breath.

"You said you know a little jazz, right?" He held up what could only be the sheet music to several songs.

"Some," she answered carefully. This guy could put her to shame without even trying.

"Let's see what you can do with these. The range isn't too demanding for you. It should be a nice gentle warm-up for more challenging pieces later."

He put the music into her hands and turned her back toward the practice studio.

She was still standing there when he sat at the piano. He glanced over his shoulder, a curious frown on his face.

"Shasta...What's wrong?"

She flipped through the first song, one page after another, and stared at the music. The notes were as intelligible as a Chinese newspaper. Her secret was out. She heard the *whoosh* of her rushing bloodstream in her ears. There was no way she could fake it with him. Damn.

His eyes widened as the truth dawned on him. "You've gotta be kidding?"

Giving him a pained smile, she shrugged. "I wish."

"But you're in a band. You play bass guitar. How did you get where you are without knowing how to read music?"

Shasta cringed with shame. "I snuck in the back?"

"No, no way." He slumped where he sat and stared at her.

"Hey! Don't give me that look. Not everyone gets to go to *Julliard*. Most of us are stuck with public schools where they cut music programs and shit like that the minute money gets tight. Welcome to *my* world."

Shasta stomped over to the piano and slapped

the sheet music down on top of it. She didn't expect Blake to grab her by the wrist before she could move away. The awkward moment seemed to stretch on—though in reality it was likely only seconds—while he studied her as she fidgeted on the inside. She broke eye contact and focused on those long fingers of his, easily circling her wrist and overlapping his thumb from the opposite side. Her skin began to tingle and radiate warmth beginning at their point of contact. She wanted to stoke her anger, but the furious heat shifted on her in an unexpected and alarming way. It was impossible to mistake the change in the energy between them when she looked at him again.

She could physically feel his eyes roaming her face. When he lingered on her mouth she held her breath. His gaze returned to hers and to her surprise, there was contrition in his tone.

"I'm sorry. It just means we have a little more work to do, that's all." He drew her down, next to him, scooting over on the bench to give her room. "Wait here."

Without another word, he was up and through the back door again.

She barely had time to tinker at the keys before he returned with a plastic template and a pencil.

"What is that?"

"I've had this thing...I don't even know how long. Check this out." He opened it up and pressed it flat against the wood behind the keyboard.

Every key was labeled. "Notes."

"A, b, c, d, e," he sang each as he struck the corresponding key. She joined him for the rest of the scale and they both smiled at the end.

Shasta chuckled. "Cool."

"It is," he agreed and pulled the sheet music off the top of the pile and opened it in front of them. "Show me what you *do* know, and we'll take it from there."

As it turned out, she knew more than she realized and she was a quick study. At the end of the session, he insisted on sending her home with the song they'd worked on the longest so she could review their lesson and all the notes he'd written on the sheet music.

Her biggest surprise came when Blake rose and said, "If you're not in any hurry, come on back." He nodded toward the door leading to his personal digs.

"Really?"

"Sure, why not?"

"I don't know." Shasta got up and followed him through the door. She came to a stop and simply stared at her surroundings. "Holy shit," she murmured.

He disappeared into the kitchen on the right, but she kept on walking. Every step felt like she was sinking into the carpet by inches.

Blake's two cream-colored leather sofas faced each other with a beautiful old Indian rug between them. The walls were a matte sage green. The wide baseboards and moldings around the doors and windows were painted the same cream to match the sofas, but the windows themselves were stained deep brown, like the wood furnishings, and picked up the color woven into the ornate rug. There was a lone forest green club chair in the far corner, a small reading table and floor lamp beside to it.

The few groupings of pictures on the walls were black and white close-ups of instruments, the dark frames bordering a deeper green than the walls. She could see the bridge of a violin in one, the gleam of a sax in another. An old mandolin with a crack hung on the wall nearby.

"Do you drink milk?" Blake asked, peeking out through the open doorway.

"Yes."

The question barely registered as she wandered over to the built-in fireplace. She ran her hand along the satin-smooth mantle, appreciating the crafts–manship that had gone into this place. There were logs in the hearth, but that meant nothing in these old buildings. Lots of chimneys were closed up. "Does this thing work?" she called to him.

"What thing?" he hollered back. She heard what could only be the fridge closing.

"Fireplace."

"Oh. Yes."

"Hmm." Tinkling? Did she just hear tinkling and crackling? What was he doing?

A black baby grand stood near the windows to her left, the natural light muted by partially closed blinds. Gliding over to the piano, she noted the wear of the keys. This was a well used instrument with a history of its own. Overall, there was a sense of dignity and calm to the apartment, very much in keeping with the grand old building itself, which was still regal, if no longer fashionable. She liked it. It suited him.

"Shasta?"

Blake motioned her over to the dining room table. A plate of Oreos—a*ha,* now the *crackling* and *tinkling* made sense—and two glasses of milk were waiting. One was set at the foot of the table, the other to the left of it. *Okay.* She left him the chair at the end and drew the other out for herself.

He sat down and they both reached for a cookie at the exact same time, each pulling instantly back.

He chuckled and nodded to the plate. "Go

ahead."

"Thanks." Shasta took two cookies, feeling more skittish and out of place than ever. What was she doing here? Why had he asked her over?

He helped himself to a cookie then watched her dunk hers into the milk.

"What?" she snapped. The needles and pins were getting unbearable.

His grin spread slowly, but it was devastating. "Nothing. You're full of surprises. That's all. How long have you been playing guitar?"

She thought back as she swished her next bite in the cold milk, flecked with dark crumbs. "I'm not sure. One of my mom's *friends* left the guitar and I just sort of picked it up, started messing around. It was something to do. The next thing I know I'm trying to imitate what I hear on the stereo."

His muted chuckle was warm; the smile that went with it flattering to her ego. "Bet you could play the piano the same way."

With a shrug of nonchalance, she admitted, "I haven't had much chance to find out." Shasta slipped into a memory. "There was this guy who used to play with my mom. He'd let me mess around on the piano a few times before they got started." Her eyes refocused on Blake and she explained. "When I was little, my mom would sometimes drag me along to rehearsals. The bars were usually pretty empty at that time of day so she'd put me at an out–of–the–way table with a Shirley Temple and my books. If I was good, I'd get maraschino cherries on a sword. I used to collect them—swords, that is. And umbrellas," she added with a grin.

Blake smiled and twisted his next Oreo apart. "Sarah mentioned your mom is a singer."

Shasta's entire body stiffened up. "Technically speaking."

He frowned. "What does that mean?"

"Condensed version? My mom's a functioning alcoholic lounge singer by day and a sloppy drunk when she stumbles home at night—*if* she goes home at all. I was cleaning up her messes when I was eight. By the time I was ten, I didn't want her to come home anymore because she created more work and liked to bring strange guys with her."

"What did you do?"

"I was a kid. What *could* I do? I'd lock my bedroom door. In the morning, I'd brew a pot of strong coffee, put out a bottle of aspirin, and take off before sleeping beauty and the beast du jour dragged themselves out of bed."

"And that's how you got your guitar."

"Bingo." She slowly scraped the frosting off

another cookie with her top teeth.

He stared down the long table, his expression grave. "Here I thought *I* had it rough."

The corner of her mouth twisted into a cynical smirk. "You? Give me a break. My mother basically abandoned me by age fourteen. She hit the road, left a small stash of cash in the cookie jar, and expected me to survive on that until she got back. I learned pretty damn quick how to stretch a buck."

"Parents," he muttered in disgust.

She scoffed at that. "Like *you* have anything to complain about. I've read your bio. Talk about being born with a silver spoon in your mouth."

To her surprise, a strange look passed over his face and he dropped back in his chair, as if he simply didn't have the energy to sit up straight anymore. It unnerved her.

"Things aren't always what they seem from the outside, Shasta."

She rubbed her bicep, suddenly chilled. "You're starting to spook me. They didn't beat you or something, did they?"

His soft laugh fell flat and he stared at the edge of the table in front of him. His words, when they came, were a dull monotone. "They barely looked at me."

Shasta felt the suppressed pain in that simple

statement. She knew it well, recognized it in herself. "Sounds like we have more in common than we realized. Fucking parents."

Blake chuckled into his hand, the corner of his smile spreading beyond his curled fingers. "You're a colorful young woman."

"You want me to sugarcoat it?"

"Heaven forbid." Then his head dropped back and he laughed in earnest, his bared throat looking more tantalizing than any neck should.

Shasta shook herself back to sanity and ventured forth on the uncomfortable subject plaguing her lately. "Mind if I ask you something?"

Returning to himself, he seemed to consider her question for a beat. "Go ahead."

"Can I...is it even possible to go back to singing with *Velvet Bitches*?"

He toyed with the base of his glass, silently watching her. "I guess that decision is up to you."

Shasta threw up her arms in exasperation. "What a cop out."

His left brow arched slightly. "I'm not here to direct your career. All I'm supposed to do is help you learn how to use your voice so you'll *have* one."

There was a heavy weight of responsibility and expectation pressing on her chest. It made her next words sound muted and weak, as if she couldn't get enough breath behind them. Maybe she couldn't. "But everyone wants that raw, gritty sound."

"That's not your natural voice." A simple truth with awful repercussions.

She clutched the back of her head with both hands and groaned. "I know, but that's the band. That's the kind of music we play."

"Then go sing it that way. You don't need me to tell you that they're going to end up replacing you eventually, anyway. You can't keep it up."

Shasta grumbled and slumped down in her chair, the edge of her thick-soled boot knocking repeatedly against the leg of the chair across from her. "Shit!" There was impotent rage and violence in that whisper but damn it, she was frustrated. "This sucks."

♫

Blake studied his young protégé and felt the stirrings of compassion. He didn't envy her position. It was as if the world had pulled the rug out from under her just when she'd gotten to her feet. She turned her bleak eyes on him and he knew the emotions she couldn't manage to shield from him were costing her. Something told him she'd been hiding her feelings for a long time.

Like recognized like. They'd both bluffed their way through life, pretending to be harder than they were, resistant and resilient. When he was younger, he'd been on intimate terms with that coping mechanism.

From where he was sitting, Shasta's vulnerability made her more compelling. She'd finally stepped out of character and become a living, breathing human being.

"Have you talked to them about it?" he finally asked, confident he knew the answer.

"No," she grumbled. "I know I have to, but I keep putting it off. I hate knowing I'm letting them down." She squeezed her eyes shut and expelled a heavy sigh. "They're not just my friends, they're my family."

The flash of pain in her eyes when she peeked at him was unmistakable.

"They kept my secrets. You have no idea. When my mom was on the road and the money was gone, they'd sneak me food so I wouldn't go hungry. Social services would have taken me away if any of them spilled the beans, but they always covered for me after Frank died."

"Frank?"

"I don't want to talk about it."

Blake lifted his hands, backing away from the

sensitive subject.

There had to be something he could do. She'd had a shitty mother, hard and lonely childhood, lost some guy named Frank, and now she was afraid of losing the girls who'd always had her back. The kid needed someone discreet and impartial in her corner, a person who could listen with compassion and give her objective guidance. *Of course!*

He shot to his feet so fast he nearly upset his chair. "Come on," he said, giving Shasta an eager nod.

Clearly puzzled, she rose slowly, warily. "Where are we going?"

"Someplace special."

Chapter Five

"You're driving me nuts. What's the big secret?" Shasta scowled at Blake as they pushed through the turnstiles to the subway platform. He wasn't listening to her.

"I hope she checks her messages." He slid his phone into his pocket. "She hates surprises."

"Who? Are you listening to me?"

He ignored the question and drove her forward, perfectly aware she was getting frustrated and annoyed with him. Strange guy. Then, without a word, without any warning whatsoever, he grabbed the back of Shasta's coat and lifted her. She felt her feet leave the ground as he hoisted her onto the train ahead of him. She yanked free, smoothed her coat back down, and gave him a sharp look for the unnecessary manhandling.

"Do you *mind*? Hands off the leather."

Unfazed by her pissy tone, Blake looked over her head and scoped out the train as he hustled her along. "We should find a seat."

The guy was impossible.

"Go ahead. Ignore me." She flapped her arms in irritation and kept walking, herded along against her will.

The train made a violent lurch and Shasta fell back against him. Blake caught her around the waist, righting her. Startled by his unexpected support, she spun and reached for the nearest pole. They both grabbed it at the same time, their hands connecting on cold metal. His eyebrows shot up at the skin contact. Thrown by it herself, she carefully eased her hand out from under his, creating a little space between them. That's when she realized, his left hand was still on her waist.

Her eyes narrowed. "You can't avoid touching me, can you?"

His cheek twitched as if she'd amused him. "Sorry."

She didn't buy it. Sincere apologies didn't usually come with cocky smiles. Still, when he dropped his arm, she felt like kicking herself.

As they picked up speed, he quietly watched the windows while her eyes darted everywhere but up at him. She fought hard to ignore his hand wrapped around the pole in front of her. The open vee of his collar was a distraction she did not need in her life. She pretended total indifference to how their bodies shook and swayed in tandem with the motion of the train. Only her circulatory system knew the truth. She was far too aware of the guy.

This was no good. She closed her eyes,

breathed in through her nose, out through her mouth, hoping to bring her circulatory system back under control. To her consternation, when her lashes flickered open, brown eyes met deep gray. He'd been watching her. *Awkward.*

The subway slowed and Shasta rocked against him. "Oh shit. Sorry," she said, righting herself.

"No harm done, Shasta. Relax."

"Easy for you to say. You know where you're going," she muttered.

He chuckled. "I want you to meet someone."

"That's *it*?"

"That's it," he confirmed with an agreeable smile.

"Why didn't you say so?"

♫

Blake wondered the same thing. He honestly couldn't say why he was being closed-lipped. Ordinarily, he didn't appreciate games, but he'd come to like it when she messed with him. He enjoyed her lip, her off-color asides, even her targeted zingers. It was satisfying to be able to give a little back and keep her guessing.

As they were jolted and jostled on their journey, he noticed she was avoiding eye contact with him. He wasn't sure why, but it allowed him to examine her more closely. Fresh faced, she was actually quite attractive. Not that he'd ever be interested in someone her age. Still, there was no denying her natural beauty now that she'd left off wearing war paint to their sessions. He was glad she'd stopped spiking her bangs too. Her hair looked soft and touchable.

He realized he was smiling as he moved on to her ears. The girl liked her piercings. She'd shot a pair of onyx posts through the holes just above the small silver hoops curled around each lobe. It looked nice, but his attention swept back to the tiny diamond stud in her left nostril, so small you could easily overlook it in passing. He certainly had—initially. Much to his surprise, he found it downright sexy now. Admiring the alluring face before him, he wondered idly what she was currently wearing in her navel. Had she pierced anything else? Pondering the tantalizing possibilities, a sudden and troubling thought occurred to him.

"Please tell me you didn't pierce your tongue."

His comment brought her head up sharply and she scowled at him, her wariness and confusion crystal clear.

"*What*?"

"You have a lot of piercings," he explained. "It's a valid question."

The kid probably killed at cards with that poker face. "That wasn't a question."

He gave her a fixed, patient stare. Shasta heaved a heavy sigh and opened her mouth, slowly rolling out her perfect, unblemished pink tongue.

Christ almighty.

His grip on the pole tightened. It would have been a gross understatement to say Blake was thrown by her action, and his subsequent reaction. His breath came fast and shallow. There were sudden heat blooms under his arms and across his torso, and he felt a stirring in the front of his jeans he didn't want to acknowledge.

"Are you satisfied?" she asked, her sultry alto kicking him when he was down.

"A simple yes or no would have sufficed," he told her dryly. "This is our stop. Come on."

♫

Shasta bounded up the steps and into daylight one step behind Blake. He cut left, went around a couple of tourists examining a subway map, and urged her forward with an impatient wave.

The guy had energy to burn. Amusing. If she hadn't seen his face flush red when she'd flashed him her tongue, she wouldn't have believed it. She'd actually embarrassed him. *Wicked.*

Hurrying to keep abreast of him, she grumbled, "Where's the fire?"

He glanced at her and checked his stride. "Sorry."

"Yeah, well these shoes weren't made for running."

"Why do you wear them?"

"I like 'em."

He scoffed at her footwear and she sneered back.

Ignoring her, Blake pulled his phone out of his pocket and placed another call. "Oh good. You're there." He sighed. "We're right outside." He broke into a chuckle. "That's not necessary. Be right up. Buzz us in, okay?"

He cut the call and headed up a short flight of steps to a heavy wooden door with a thick security glass window. The buzzer sounded and he pulled the door open and waved Shasta through. She took in the modest interior, wondering again who they could possibly be visiting—certainly not his girlfriend, the stunning, Valerie Walters. She could afford better.

When they stepped off the elevator, Blake grabbed Shasta by the shoulder of her coat and tugged her to the left, his sideways nod pointing the way as he paced down the hallway.

Shasta swatted his hand away and smoothed her coat, *again*, shifting her shoulders so it hung properly. "Knock that shit off! Final warning— hands off the leather."

He gave her a mysterious smile and, reaching back, snapped his fingers right under her chin. Shasta's head jerked up in surprise. Her eyes narrowed on the man. He was having way too much fun messing with her.

Oh, this was so much better than being pawed — not!

"And we were getting along so nicely, too," she muttered and just about collided with Blake when he stopped short at the next door.

It opened before he could knock.

You could have knocked Shasta over with a feather when Blake embraced the elderly woman in front of them. The tender kiss he planted on her forehead wasn't for show. The woman's affectionate laugh as she hugged him back was equally genuine. These two were happy to see each other.

"This is a pleasant surprise," said the old woman.

Blake shifted to her side, his arm wrapped possessively around her delicate shoulders. With a grin Shasta couldn't begin to understand, he nodded at her and said, "Clara, I'd like you to meet Shasta Kovich."

Shasta could almost swear she saw the old woman's face fall for a second there. *Oh great.* However, she recovered instantly. Her gray eyebrows rose a little higher and the corners of her mouth twitched. "Like the composer?"

Blake chuckled. "Certainly seems so."

The old lady looked up at him and shook her head. Her blue eyes were twinkling. "You had me going there for a second."

He grinned. "I know what you thought. Not happening." Releasing her, he took a step back.

The old woman turned her smile on Shasta. "Please, come in. Like he said, I'm Clara."

"Hi, Clara. Thank you."

Shasta followed Clara into the apartment, giving Blake a queer glance on the way by. He closed the door and trailed them into the cozy living room.

"Please, have a seat—anywhere *but* the rocker," said their hostess.

"It's easier for Clara to get in and out of the rocker," Blake explained, giving the old lady a loving smile.

So, the guy does know how to charm. Interesting.

Shasta eased down on the striped easy chair. If she had to label the colors, she'd say they were rose and ivory. Rather than take the remaining chair, Blake put his arm around Clara and led her to the rocker, his manner caring and protective. She had no choice but to sit.

"Don't worry about offering us anything from the kitchen," he told her. "We just had milk and cookies. We're fine. Can I get *you* anything?"

"I'm fine, dear." Only now did he take the last chair. Clara turned her smile back to Shasta. "This is nice. Blake never brings me visitors." The old lady raised her eyebrows at him, inviting an explanation.

He settled back in the old wing chair, crossed his foot over his knee, and smiled. "I'm doing voice work with Shasta."

Shasta had a tendency to crack her knuckles when she was nervous. She was right in the middle of doing just that when she realized they were watching her. Busted, she grimaced apologetically at their hostess. "Sorry. Bad habit." She tucked her hands under her legs. "Um, I'm in a band," she offered, joining the conversation.

Clara nodded, her mouth shifting to hold back a smile.

"She had vocal cord surgery so we're strengthening her voice," he continued.

"Oh." Clara might as well have said, "What a shame," the way her words and face fell. Her soft, blue eyes cut back and forth between her young visitors then finally settled on Shasta again. "And the purpose of your visit?"

Shasta gave her a clueless shrug and both women laughed.

Blake scratched his head. "I was hoping you'd still have my old beginner piano books hanging around."

"Those old things?" She broke into a soft chuckle. "You know I do. Why do you ask?"

"Shasta doesn't read music."

Clara stared in amazement. "You don't—"

Shasta cringed, deeply embarrassed all over again. "I never learned."

"But…you're in a *band*," persisted the old lady, obviously trying to understand how that could be.

"I taught myself."

"By ear," Blake added. "She has natural talent, Clara. But she needs to know how to read sheet music if she's going to survive. This goes way beyond what I'm supposed to be doing with her. I think it would be best if we kept this between ourselves. Shasta's got a career to protect."

"I see. Yes, I think you're probably right," said Clara.

"We could use your help, if you're up to it." Uncrossing his leg, Blake sat forward, his elbows on his knees, hands clasped in front of him.

"Well," Clara broke off, considering it. "I don't play like I used to. You know that."

"You don't have to. I want *her* to play." He tipped his head sideways in Shasta's direction.

Shasta straightened up in her chair and stared at him. "Me? I play guitar."

"I don't expect you to become a concert pianist, but it will help you learn the fundamentals."

The women looked at one another.

Shasta was game. "What do you think?"

Clara slowly nodded then broke into a smile. "It'll be nice to feel useful again. Why not?"

"Thank you." If these two could bring her up to speed, and keep her secret, she'd owe them her undying gratitude.

"Great." Blake clapped his hands and shot out of his chair. "I'll leave you two to work out the details, okay?"

"You're leaving?" both women asked at exactly the same time.

Amused, he broke into a little laugh. "I have an engagement. I have to go." He looked at his wristwatch then back at Shasta. "I'll see you in a couple of days." Bending down, he kissed Clara on the top of the head. "I'll see *you* Friday." Heading toward the door he called over his shoulder, "Work on your breathing, Shasta."

Clara turned to her, undoubtedly baffled by his directive.

Shasta rolled her eyes. "Long story."

Chapter Six

Short on time, Blake hailed a cab and raced to the theater. With any luck, Val wouldn't be ready. There was a small crowd gathered on the sidewalk outside when he hopped out of the vehicle. Vijay saw him through the glass and opened one of the locked theater doors for him.

He gave Vijay a nod of thanks. The doorman's parting words followed him toward the interior doors ahead. "They're running late today."

"Good."

Blake pushed his way into the stylishly modern theater and winced at the sharp tone in Valerie's voice. The excellent acoustics ensured not a whisper of her ugly mood would be missed. He stopped walking and hovered in the shadows of the back rows.

Wonderful. Another pleasant evening ahead.

As he watched, cast and crew were quietly slinking away, one after another, presumably to avoid drawing fire themselves from the diva in full rant. He scratched the back of his head, dropped heavily into the nearest seat on his right, and stretched his long legs into the aisle. Astonishingly, it only took seconds for Valerie to ramp up his tension. The woman wore him out—and not in a good way. He kicked back and closed his eyes, making deep, penetrating circles between his brows with his thumb, hoping to keep another Val-induced headache at bay.

Expelling an exhausted sigh, he let his arm fall to the back of the next seat and looked around. His gaze lit on the floor of the balcony overhead, the numerous rows of seats in every direction, the suspended stage lights, the curtains, the orchestra pit, even the floor lights. He looked at everything except Val. There was nothing more unattractive than seeing her behave like this. She'd learned early her tantrums didn't work on him. Still, it curdled his stomach to see her go ballistic on others. She was a spoiled woman, full of her own consequence, convinced the hype didn't do her justice in the talent department.

What the hell am I doing here?

He wasn't entirely sure why he was wasting time with this woman. From the outside, it might seem a ridiculous thing to ponder. After all, she was a beauty. Add her gorgeous figure to the face and it wasn't hard to believe the stories of men getting whiplash when she walked by. Val knew how to make love to both a camera and an audience. She wasn't nearly as warm and beguiling to those behind the scenes. Anyone working in theater she couldn't handle, she'd bully. Temperamental and harsh at times, she was forgiven over and over again by her fans and the press for conduct he found increasingly inexcusable.

He wondered what poor soul was in her crosshairs tonight. Probably another understudy. For a vain woman, Valerie was easily threatened and paranoid of rivals. She could be vicious and cruel to those she saw as competition.

His mind slipped to how their quasi-relationship began. They were passing acquaint—tances for nearly a year before they finally had an actual conversation. He found her lively, engaging—charming. Val knew how to impress those she chose to impress. She initiated more when she phoned to ask if he could be her plus-one for an upcoming wedding. He agreed. Two more invitations followed and he was fine when people took him as her de facto escort. Half the time, he was planning to attend the same function anyway. He still remembered the cab ride back to her place after a star-studded movie premier. He was quietly admiring her profile when she turned and touched his face. They both moved in for that first kiss. In all honesty, it thrilled him at the time. This was an exceptional woman, or so it seemed. He didn't know yet she was the sort of person who could run over a puppy with her car and get angry at the puppy for screwing up her day. She let those little sides of her stellar personality out in tiny doses, easily explained away and forgiven.

That night in the cab was when they shifted from friends to friends-with-benefits. He wasn't in love with her, nor was he afraid she was at risk in that regard, but they each answered a need in the other. His was to keep her unwelcome admirers at bay and—while not ideal or particularly warm—she managed to chase away the deep loneliness that sometimes hit him like a sledgehammer. Just sharing a bed with another person was enough to banish the emptiness back to the shadows and allow him to sleep. Or it used to be. Even that wasn't working anymore.

He felt emotionally detached whenever he looked at her. It was worse when they slept together. Sex had become a performance, so unsatisfying he felt relief when intimacy was over and he could slip away, make a drink, and numb the despair he felt afterwards. He'd never thought life would be this bland, this colorless.

Music was the exception.

Closing his eyes, he brought the image of Val into mental focus. Considering she was a natural, gifted actress, he honestly couldn't tell if anything about her was genuine or not. He hoped she was just going through the motions, like he was. He'd rather not hurt her. Frankly, it was more palatable to believe he was merely a convenience too. He was an acceptable escort and a safe lover. With clout of his own, and general acceptance in his parents' elite circles, he'd opened doors that wouldn't automatically admit her otherwise.

He snorted softly. *Get over yourself, Adams.* Maybe all it came down to was looking decent enough in a tux when the cameras were flashing. She loved to put her best foot forward, and the right arm candy was important to her. He'd known that for some time.

Pushing his thoughts aside, Blake returned to the present. Only now did he notice he was alone. Hauling himself up, he made his way to the back of the stage and Val's dressing room. He and the director passed one another in the corridor. The director's face and ears were deep red, his mouth a tight line, jaw clenched, and eyes hard. Not a good sign. Their argument must have just ended.

The man spun around and caught Blake's arm. "Take her home...and keep her there." His voice shook with barely controlled anger. Blake gave him a firm nod. A look of perfect understanding passed between them. The director shook his head and strode away muttering to himself.

Val's dressing room was two doors down on the right. Blake paused in front of it, giving himself a moment to brace for whatever was about to hit before giving the door a light rap with the back of his hand.

"Val?"

"It's open."

She was sitting at her vanity, violently brushing her gleaming, copper hair with long strokes, working out her temper on her curls.

No way was he going to raise the issue that upset her. It would come out soon enough.

"You're late," she snapped.

"Barely. You weren't ready anyway." He dropped against the wall, leaning on his shoulder in order to study her flawless profile.

"Did you hear?" She spared a quick glance at him.

He played dumb. "Hear what?"

"Gordon wants me to sit out tonight. He thinks I need a break and Olivia's earned another evening performance." Valerie threw her hairbrush and it upset a container of powder, sending peach-colored talc over everything. "Damn it!" She leaped to her feet, shaking and close to furious tears.

He grabbed her hand and pulled her into his arms, massaging circles on her back. "Hey now, calm down."

"I know what they're doing," she said into his shoulder, and gripped his jacket with both fists.

"Shh." Pacifying her had become his primary role, one he didn't particularly enjoy. Val's arms slipped to his waist and he felt the tension slowly ease from her body.

When she stepped away, she wore a more resolute expression. Her perfect mask was in place. "But this isn't over."

The hairs on the back of his neck stood on end. "Val, let it go. For now. We're going to miss our reservation if we don't hurry."

He grabbed her jacket and held it up so she could slip into it. Copper curls whipped him in the face when she pulled her hair free of the collar. Turning, she noticed him rubbing the inside corner of his eye.

"What's the matter?"

"Nothing."

Skeptical, she studied him for a moment before breaking her silence with an alternate proposal. "Or…" Her sharp, polished fingernails walked slowly up his chest and over his shoulder. The fiery seductress had returned. "We could just skip dinner and go straight to my place."

He caught her wrist and carefully moved her hand before she could pull him down for a kiss, hiding his motive behind an insincere smile. "I was looking forward to dinner." That was a lie, but it beat the truth.

"Fine." She stroked his cheek instead, a pensive look in her eye, and a determined set to her lovely mouth. "We'll go there afterwards. I hope you're planning to stay the night."

Blake turned into her hand and kissed the inside of her wrist. It wasn't an answer, but she accepted it as one. He let her.

♫

Shasta gnawed her lower lip while she butchered Twinkle, Twinkle Little Star. This was downright painful.

Without warning, Clara struck the top of her hand. "Stop that!"

Shasta jerked back from the keys in surprise. "What the hell?"

Clara scowled. "You're not listening to me." Clearly aggrieved, she expelled a heavy sigh. "Use *all* your fingers. What are you doing? Let's go back to practicing scales."

"Oh come on," Shasta groaned. "Let's not, and

say we did."

Clara's brow arched in challenge. "Then prove you've been paying attention."

Shasta blew out a huffy breath and glared right back for an extended beat. The battle of wills ended when she returned her hand to the keys and played the scales they'd worked on over and over again without a single hitch.

"There, you see? You did *that* right. How come you change when we move on to music?"

Baffled, Shasta threw up her hands. "I don't know."

"You need to work on your fingering some more. Do you have a piano or a keyboard at home?"

"No, but I'm pretty sure I can get my hands on one." Miri must have something she could borrow.

"Good." Clara closed the music book in front of them and handed it to Shasta. "Take this home and practice thirty minutes a day. An hour would be better."

"Does this mean we're done?" Hope flared at the thought.

"For now. You weren't half-bad for your first day, Shasta. I expect you to come back in a few days and show me your progress. Now, how about some tea?"

"I'd love some tea."

"I'll go put on the kettle."

Clara made her slow and careful way into the kitchen, ignoring the cane hanging off the arm of her rocker. Shasta watched her go, amused the old woman was as stubborn and rebellious as she was.

Setting the practice book on top of her coat, Shasta wandered over to the built-in shelves to look at pictures. There were a lot of them. The ones that interested her most were obviously of Blake. Frame after frame showed his evolution from young boy to grown man. No acne. No braces. No seriously bad hair days in any of the photos. Shasta might have hated him if it weren't for the irregular smile in one of the earlier pictures where his adult teeth were still growing in. Apparently no one earned a pass through that awkward stage. Good.

"It'll just be a minute," Clara said from the doorway behind her.

Shasta looked around with a grin and pointed to the numerous photos. "Doesn't take a bad picture, does he?"

Clara laughed. "I haven't seen one, but then, I love him."

"I still can't believe you were his nanny. I've never known anyone with a nanny before."

Shasta's gaze returned to the shelf and she picked up what looked like the most recent photo. In this one, Clara was seated and there was a colorful present on her lap. Blake was leaning over her, hugging her from behind, caught in the act of giving the old lady a kiss on the cheek. The smile of delight on Clara's face was priceless. Because there was no way it was posed, the candid photo struck Shasta as particularly sweet.

She turned it, showing it to her hostess. "I like this one."

Clara's smile softened. "It's one of my favorites."

"I bet you don't think anyone's good enough for him, huh?"

"Oh...I think there's someone out there for everyone."

Focused on the photo in her hand, Shasta felt the uncomfortable flash of attraction return. The sadness that instantly followed was even stronger, penetrating deep. No matter how far back she went, she couldn't remember anyone ever looking at her with such open adoration and love.

Swallowing the lump in her throat, she glanced up at Clara. "Do you think Valerie Walters is the one? For Blake?"

Why was she so curious? Talk about fishing.

Clara looked troubled. "I've never met the woman. I couldn't say."

After carefully replacing the picture, Shasta turned back in confusion. "Seriously? That's weird."

"What is, dear?"

"He brought *me* here. I've only known him a few weeks."

Clara smiled. "Clearly you're a special case."

Shasta snorted. "Yeah, head case maybe."

The shrill whistle from the kitchen interrupted Clara's reply. Instead, she beckoned Shasta into the next room. "Come. The kettle's hot and the table is ready."

They sat at the small kitchen table, a plate of lemon butter cookies in front of them, and simply talked. Shasta didn't expect to tell the old lady so much of her personal history. It just happened. A single innocuous question and the next thing she knew, one detail tumbled into the next, and knocked down another. Like dominoes falling, she'd started a chain reaction. Shasta told her about being hungry sometimes and scared most of the time. Now Clara knew Shasta still slept with a battered aluminum baseball bat next to her bed for protection. Most of all, Clara knew about the people Shasta loved most—her band mates and Frank.

"The record collection Frank left you sounds valuable."

Already emotionally stirred, her feelings close

to the surface, Shasta reacted forcefully and firmly to the observation. "I'd never sell it."

"Of course not." Clara calmed her with a reassuring pat on the hand. "I'd never suggest such a thing. I'm just thinking of what you've got there. It's history."

Contrite and embarrassed, Shasta looked down at the table and mumbled, "I'm sorry. It's just that, well, so many people only care about how much something is worth." She chanced a look at Clara and found the older woman nodding slowly. "They don't care about the true value. You know what I mean?"

"More than you know."

Shasta laughed at the words and broke out singing the lyrics for '*More than you know.*' Clara clasped her hands in delight, her face lit up.

"How wonderful! Oh, Blake was right. You have a beautiful voice," Clara told Shasta when she fell silent.

The compliment made Shasta glow from the inside out and she grinned, her smile bigger than ever. "Just don't tell Blake I did that, okay? He'd probably freak because he wasn't here to approve every note or something stupid like that."

Clara chuckled softly. "Is he tough to work with?"

Thinking about it before she answered, Shasta was forced to admit, "He started out that way, but I understand why he pushed me so hard. My notes are longer and stronger now. He's taught me a lot." Shasta leaned in and whispered conspiratorially, "Don't tell him that, either, okay?"

Clara's tempered amusement gave way to an uninhibited laugh. "Okay."

Shasta took another cookie then slumped back in her chair. Brooding on her conversation with Blake earlier, she rubbed the rough granules of sugar with the pad of her thumb before taking a bite. "He told me about his childhood. A little anyway."

Clara appeared to be startled when she looked up at her.

The old lady opened her mouth as if to say something, stopped herself, then lightly stroking her ear, she tried again. "What did he say, dear?"

The strange lump in Shasta's throat had nothing to do with the cookie she just swallowed. She grabbed her cup of tepid tea and finished what was left. Only then could she get out the words. Why did they feel so important, so weighty? "Just that he was invisible to them."

To Shasta's surprise, a flash of pain and heartache crossed Clara's face. The old woman picked up her folded napkin and carefully wiped up the crumbs in front of her, closing them inside the napkin. Shasta knew what she was doing. When she was anxious, she had a tendency to tidy things too. Clara's eyes were clear when they landed on Shasta, but the sadness remained.

"Blake wasn't even five when I was hired and yet, there'd already been a handful of nannies through his life." She sniffed softly, wringing her hands in her lap. "He didn't speak for the first month—kept his distance and a wary eye on me. I couldn't coax him close. I'd never seen a more...*self-contained* child in my life. He was obedient—always picked up his toys when asked and ate whatever I put in front of him. He'd look through books I knew he couldn't read, but wouldn't share them with me so I could read them to him. It was so odd. I'd never cared for a child like him. I thought he was emotionally stunted in some way until I saw the most heartbreaking thing, and realized how I'd misjudged him."

Clara picked up her cup, noticed it was empty, and set it down again. There was a soft clatter when it hit her spoon. No doubt she needed a moment to collect her thoughts. Finally composed, she explained, "Blake's parents had been away, in London for over two months. They came back unannounced. We both heard the front door and

Blake ran downstairs as fast as he could. I still remember his excited, happy little face. I'd never seen him smile before. I chased after him and was there when he reached the newel post at the bottom. His parents had just finished hanging their coats in the front closet when they turned and noticed him." Clara fell silent, blinking, her eyes, even now, decades later, glittering with tears.

Shasta sat forward, anxious and upset herself without knowing why. "What happened?"

Clara's feeble smile trembled at the corners. "They looked right at him and frowned. His mother actually said, 'Blake, what are you doing down here? Where's your nanny? Go to your nanny.' I'm not even sure she remembered my name at the time. Blake's father patted him on the head on his way to the living room, asking his wife over his shoulder if he should pour her a sherry, too."

The old woman's fragile frame seemed to sink in on itself, as if protecting her heart from the pain. "And that was it. After eight weeks, they were back with barely a glance in Blake's direction. No hugs. No kisses. No, 'We missed you, honey.' Not even a gift to buy him off for their neglect. That's when it dawned on me they'd never once asked to speak with him during their rare phone calls."

Shasta was appalled. "Those shits!"

"My sentiments exactly. It took me three hours to coax Blake out of his closet. He'd been quietly crying in there. I sat up in his bed the entire night, holding him while he slept." She dashed at her eyes with a corner of her napkin and shook her head. "No child ever hugged me quite like that. That's when I knew how much this little boy needed me. He didn't have anyone else. Never any love. I finally understood his detachment, that irritating distance. He was afraid to trust anyone after so much disappointment."

Shasta remembered his softly spoken words back at his apartment—*things aren't always what they seem*. He was right about that. She wasn't the only one with a sob story. "I'm glad you stayed with him."

"He was *my* little boy after that. Mine."

Shasta frowned again, recalling Clara's admission that she'd never met Valerie Walters. "Do you—? Never mind, forget it."

"No chance of that now. Do I what?"

"Do you think he's in love with Valerie Walters?"

"I sincerely hope not."

That was not the answer Shasta expected. "Seriously?"

"I'm quite serious."

"How come?"

Clara pursed her lips, her brow furrowed. "You must have seen the pictures."

Shasta was perplexed. "Of course. A few anyway." No need to confess she'd spent the better part of a morning looking at all the images she could find on the internet. She'd sound like some whack-job stalker. "They look gorgeous together."

"Look at them again and you'll understand my fears for him."

"*Okay*," said Shasta slowly, still confused.

Chapter Seven

There were five text messages waiting for her when Shasta hit the sidewalk and turned her phone back on. Bose had left two, Miri one. No doubt the one waiting from Dee would be bitching about something, or someone. The final message was one Shasta didn't want to deal with. It came from their agent, Sarah Goldman. Though she knew it was cowardly, Shasta deleted it. Not that it helped to put unpleasant conversations off. She simply wasn't ready to talk with her agent yet. It didn't take a genius to guess Sarah was looking for a status report.

Forget it. Until Shasta talked with Blake, she didn't want to say anything and wind up accidentally contradicting him. It was bad enough she was going to have to bite the bullet and admit her singing days with Velvet Bitches was over.

Clutching the beginner music book hidden under her coat to her chest, Shasta swiped her card to board the subway. After stashing the card back into her pocket, she sent a text to Miri.

U home? OMW.

Dropping into a vacant seat just inside the train, she read Miri's message back. *Yes. CU.*

Good. She'd get something to practice on from Miri, go home, and—Shasta noticed a man staring at her a few seats down. He didn't look like one of her typical fans so she stared pointedly back, blatantly hostile. He looked away and another passenger, who'd noticed all this, shared a quick eye-roll with Shasta. Only then did she slip back into her thoughts. Okay, get a keyboard or have Miri scare one up for her, then get home and bring up more pictures on the internet. What had Clara been hinting at? She could hardly stand the suspense.

♫

The taxi pulled up in front of Val's building and Blake threw open his door and climbed out. The driver turned with a wary frown, his gaze locked on Blake as he helped Valerie out of the car. They made eye contact over the seat and Blake asked the driver to, "Please wait."

Only then did Val understand. She turned on him, anger and disappointment flashing in her eyes. "You're *leaving*? I find this out *now*?"

"I never said I'd stay."

"You let me think—"

He reached for her hand before she lashed out physically. It had happened before. "You've had a rough day. I think you should go upstairs, draw yourself a nice bubble bath, and have a little quiet time. It'll be good for you to relax."

"You condescending prick." She yanked her hand away. "Fuck you."

"We had a nice dinner," he reminded her as she stomped off to where the doorman was waiting, watching their little drama unfold.

Blake expected a backhanded gesture, a reiteration of what she'd just said to him, but she spun around and glared—raw betrayal on her distorted, yet still lovely face. "Are you seeing someone else?"

"*No!* Of course not." Blake closed the distance and pulled her against him, giving her a paternal kiss on the forehead, carefully veering away from her lips.

Unaware of his subtle deflection, she relaxed into his embrace, clutching the back of his coat. "Then why?" Her question was so soft he barely heard it over the traffic.

"Because I forgot I'd already agreed to play with the guys tonight, that's why. I'm sorry."

She sighed and stepped back, accepting his excuse. He understood accepting was a far cry from forgiving him for double-booking her. She'd be even more upset if she knew the truth.

"I'll make it up to you. I promise." How, he

didn't know. His options had never looked so bleak. They'd slept together hundreds of times. Why did he balk at the thought of another night with her? It wasn't *that* bad. It had never been bad, just *lacking*.

He'd been wondering more and more lately if he wasn't losing himself, a little at a time, by going through the motions with this woman. Theirs was a strange, non-relationship and it was wearing on him. He wanted to step back from the void. This beautiful, hot-tempered siren of the stage exhausted him in too many ways to enumerate.

"I'll call you tomorrow." He pulled her back by the hand and gave her a quick parting peck on the cheek then fled to the waiting cab.

"You'd better," Valerie called after him.

He dropped into the back seat, told the cabbie his destination, and sank into the stained upholstery, beyond caring if it was nasty or not because he was free of her for the evening.

Then he recalled Val's wounded expression, heard her unexpected question. *"Are you seeing someone else?"* He shook his head, snorting at the idea as lights whizzed past the dark windows. Where had she come up with something like that?

Unbidden, certainly unwelcome, he remem–bered how Shasta's hand felt under his on that pole. There was no forgetting how her body felt when she fell against him as the train lurched forward. When he closed his eyes, he was lost all over again in the delicate luster of her skin, the clomping of her hard-soled boots. He saw the shimmer of the diamond stud in her perfect little nose. Even now, Blake could swear he smelled Shasta's black leather jacket, hear it creak when she moved. He visualized the profiles of both Valerie and Shasta superimposed one over the other.

Blake groaned and pressed the heels of his hands into his eyes. There was no point. No matter how hard he rubbed, it wasn't deep enough to erase Shasta from his mind.

Fan-fucking-tastic.

♪

There was a good crowd at the *Back Beat* when Blake walked into the dim club. He could tell at a glance who was there for the music and who was looking for a hook-up. Jazz lovers were nodding in time with the performance. The rest were eyeing the other patrons and talking over the music. He ignored the glances straying in his direction and made his way to the front.

Hammond Struthers was flying on the bass, but he was still the first to notice and return Blake's smile. Damien chuckled, his lips breaking the seal on his mouthpiece when he saw they'd collected another stray. He lowered his cornet and waved Blake up with them. Blake hopped the edge of the raised platform and headed over to the waiting piano, nodding a greeting to Graham Meany as he brushed the drums and cymbals, his whole body in motion.

Ham finished his riff and all three of them looked at Blake. He cocked a playful eyebrow at them then took it from there, the others joined in, layering over his notes while letting Blake take the lead. He was sweating, but smiling when he finished to rousing applause.

They all broke into a laugh and Damien introduced their pianist while Blake gave his drink order to a passing server. He needed a large glass of water with a twist of lime or these hot lights were going to kill him.

Blake switched to beer at the end of their set and they all took over a large curved booth off to the side to chill and enjoy the last reverberations of the beat still kicking through their tired bodies.

"Shit man, what the hell you doin' here tonight?" asked Meany, still drumming, this time on the dark tabletop with his bare hands.

Blake rubbed his damp brow, a philosophical grin on his face. "Beat the alternative."

Damien snorted with amusement. "You ditched her? Fuck," he said, drawing out the word. Then he shook his head and his deep rumbling chuckle got them all going. "Don't get me wrong," he added, his perfect smile lighting up that corner of the booth. "She's stunning. Beautiful. But that bitch scares the fucking shit out of me."

Shaking with laughter, Blake agreed, "Me too," and raised his bottle of beer in the air.

♫

Miri wasn't alone when Shasta got to her apartment. Her friend was wearing her little bathrobe. Clearly, she'd interrupted something. Miri's boyfriend, Sam, stayed in the bedroom while she gathered up her small keyboard and wound the cord. She zipped them inside a padded travel case for Shasta.

Walking Shasta to the door, she lingered a moment to ask, "What are you up to?"

Shasta shrugged. "Just wanted to work on something, that's all."

"Fine, don't tell me." Miri gave up with a little smile. "Before you power it on, make sure the volume is turned down or you might blast your neighbors out of their beds. I've done that."

Shasta grinned. "Thanks for the warning." She pointed to the case in her hand. "I'll get it back to you."

"No rush. It's not my favorite."

"Yeah, I figured." Shasta chuckled. "I s'pose we both have things to do."

Miri glanced over her shoulder at her bedroom door, slightly ajar, and her smile grew. "Yeah. Will I see you at practice tomorrow?"

"Yep."

"Okay."

The door clicked closed behind her and Shasta heard Miri lock it as she hoisted her leather bag more securely over her shoulder and shuffled down the hall to the staircase beyond.

Of course, once she got home, she didn't plug in the keyboard. That could wait. She went over, turned on the laptop instead, and brought the numerous images of Blake back up on the screen.

Cracking open a bottle of iced tea, she settled onto the stool and moved the mouse along the table, scrolling down the page a little at a time, loving how he looked in those candid shots. There were pictures of him with a couple of other women too. She dubbed those BVs—before Val. Some showed Blake playing in various ensembles and groups. A few on his own. There were even a couple in-studio shots and she couldn't believe who he'd worked with. Then there were the stiff photos of him at functions with his high-profile parents. However, her least favorites were the couples' shots of him and Val. Holding hands, arms around waists, him looking at her. Shasta frowned. Him looking at *her*. Is this what Clara meant?

Shasta clicked on image after image and noticed something. Valerie Walters was a one-woman show. They were both smiling in the early photos. He seemed happy enough at her side. The man could pull off a suit. And a tux? Oh boy. He had that cool and sophisticated thing down pat. Funny, he probably didn't even care. It wasn't something he'd ever have to think about or practice. It was in his posture, his polish, and that aloof expression on his handsome face. But then scrolling down, she began to notice a change. Where he'd appeared good humored, even amused while she played up to the cameras and worked the crowd, in later photos he looked impatient, irritable, and sick of it all. Valerie didn't seem to notice. He was virtually invisible to her. Oh, she touched him, draped herself on him, but could this be for real? Was he just an accessory to set off her beauty? She was looking at, and laughing with, everyone *but* him.

Coming slowly to that uncomfortable realization, she disliked the woman even more. Especially now that she knew more about Blake's history. He was unhappy with Valerie. Clearly. But was he unconsciously repeating a pattern from his childhood?

Shasta dropped back in her chair and grabbed her bottle of tea. Her gaze returned to Blake's face, frozen on the glowing screen. Before she could brace against it, a wave of tenderness spread through her. She was beginning to understand him. Devoted and loving to Clara, yet still scarred by his parents' indifference. Oh god, what was she doing?

She closed the laptop, spun off the stool, and paced the short length of her little kitchen. This wasn't good. She didn't want to get any closer to that complicated and damaged man. Not really.

Against her will, the memory of him towering over her in the subway returned. The way he'd watched her, studied her had turned her emotions on end. Simply recalling it made her experience a fluttery echo of the excitement she'd felt when he lifted her, one handed, up and into the train ahead of him. She was much too aware of the man.

"Do *not* fall for this guy, you idiot!" She closed her eyes, clenched her fists, and tried like hell to resist where her thoughts were going. She failed.

Chapter Eight

Considering the poor night's sleep she got, Shasta would have preferred to stay home and work on music by herself the next morning. Too bad. She had a voice lesson at ten. Afterwards, she was expected to turn up to rehearsals. The bothersome phone calls from her agent, Sarah, were merely another irritating bonus. Shasta let them go straight to messages. She'd deal with them later…or not.

Choking down the last of her cinnamon toast, she finished her coffee and left the dishes where they sat. They could wait. She needed to get ready.

Staring at herself in the bathroom mirror, she sighed at her hair. What did she want to do with it? It was long past the shaggy, uneven stage of growing out, but she was sick of pulling it back in a ponytail. She had no imagination. Glancing at the vanity drawer, she was half tempted to cut it again, but she withdrew her hand. The electric trimmer remained silent. No, she could deal with her damn hair. It was everything else she wasn't so sure about. Out of ideas for now, she loaded up her ears with posts and hoops.

She'd eased up on makeup these days too. She still liked a light smudge of charcoal around her eyes, a coat of mascara on her lashes, and her favorite tinted lip gloss, but that was enough to call it good. Clothing, on the other hand, proved more problematic. She needed to go shopping. Blake had already seen her in what he deemed her *appropriate clothes* too many times to count. Not that she was dressing for him. *Hell no*. She didn't care what he thought. It was just something she'd noticed, that's all.

Of course, twenty minutes later, Blake added another layer on Shasta's dark mood when he snapped at her as soon as she walked into the studio.

He spun on the bench and scowled at her. "Don't you ever answer your damn phone?"

Shasta bristled. "All the fucking time. What's it to you?"

His eyes narrowed and she hesitated just inside the door.

"Sarah's been trying to reach you," he said.

"I'm aware." Shasta dropped her bag just inside the door and closed it softly behind her. "I just wanted to check with you before I tell her anything."

Blake cocked his head and a tight line appeared between his dark brows. "Check with me?"

"Yeah. She's looking for a status report."

"So give her one."

"What am I supposed to say? *You're* in charge of my progress."

He stared at her in disbelief. "Don't you dare use me as an excuse to buy yourself more time." The muscle in his cheek jerked and twitched. No question, he was annoyed with her. "I only agreed to take you on in the first place because Sarah pitched your case so strongly. She insisted you have talent. Even more importantly, a pragmatic attitude and the maturity it takes to make it in this business. I trusted her when she said you'd land on your feet no matter what came at you."

Shasta was stunned. "Sarah said that?"

"Yes."

She looked down at the piano leg, over to his ridiculously long, dark leather shoe, up his gray Dockers-clad shin and knee, everywhere *but* his face, his eyes. Releasing a heavy sigh, she shifted her weight onto her heels and tapped the hard soles of her boots together a couple of times, her brain racing in too many directions at once to help her with her next move.

"Shasta?" Even without looking up, she could tell he'd dipped down to catch her eye. "Shasta, you're avoiding *me* now too? I never pegged you for a coward."

Her head snapped up and she glared at the man. He smiled back, triumphant. "There's the spunk I was looking for."

His reaction threw her off-kilter. Her mouth opened and closed a couple of times, but nothing came. *Nothing*. Not one sharp or pithy retort leaped to mind. She would have settled for snotty in a pinch. It was futile. Faced with the reality of her situation, her false bravado and sass had fled, leaving her utterly panic-stricken. She had to tell the band, her agent, the public. They were all waiting, hovering, circling. The thought made her shudder. Suddenly she imagined herself floating in a tiny dingy, without oars, while sharks ominously lapped the small craft. This could be the end for her. Knowing that didn't make it easy to leave the boat and enter the water.

"Putting off the inevitable is only going to make things worse." His tone softened. Was that compassion, kindness? "Your friends have been patient and supportive so far, but that'll change if they find out you've kept something this important from them. Don't do that to them, Shasta. They need time to make adjustments to the group so they can get back on the road. You're holding them up."

"Don't you think I know that?" she barked back, every muscle in her body locked for a fight.

"Don't you think I'm not tortured by those thoughts day and night?" Emotionally overwrought, Shasta stumbled backwards and hit the wall. She slid slowly down to the floor, her legs a tangle in front of her. Dropping her forehead to her crooked knee, she covered her head with her arms and panted through the pain, struggling to hold herself together.

Just when it looked like she'd made it, like she truly belonged somewhere and money would no longer be an issue, she was back to square one. Her dream was fizzling before her eyes and the old familiar feeling of being alone and abandoned returned with a vengeance. It was terrifying.

But Blake was right. Her friends were going to hate her. She had to speak up, spit it out, no matter how bitter the words. They deserved to know.

There was a shuffle next to her then the brush of fabric on fabric before a large, warm hand touched her upper back. Peering out from under her elbow, she confirmed the impossible. Blake was on the floor beside her, rubbing soothing circles across her shoulders. His move was unexpected and comforting.

"I'm okay," she mumbled, head still bowed.

"I thought you were going to pass out there for a second."

She scoffed at that. "I've never fainted in my life."

"Glad to hear it."

Without even looking, she knew he'd smiled. She heard it in his voice.

♫

He didn't envy Shasta's predicament. When he saw her face drain of color as she staggered backwards, he thought she was going to hit the floor with a mighty crash. Unable to reach her in time, all he could do now was help her breathe her way back to calm.

Rubbing slow, patient circles on her upper back, he felt the sharp ridges of her shoulder blades, the hard bump protruding at the base of her neck. He traced the boney knob with his thumb before gliding up toward the nape. Just the slightest brush of his fingers under her hair released a tantalizing tropical fragrance. The scent of pomegranate made *his* head rock slightly when it hit him. Being this near to her, touching and smelling her, was making his mouth water.

Shaken by his reaction, he tried to clear his head, control his thoughts, but they were going in a disturbing direction. He didn't want to see this slight and gruff girl as a succulent treat to be plucked, or worse, devoured! Stray thoughts like that weren't helpful—to either of them. So what if he'd finally admitted he didn't want Val? Why should it make him strangely vulnerable to this creature?

Perplexed, he withdrew his hand and got to his feet. "We're on the clock here. Are you ready to work?"

She looked up and nodded. He was relieved to see her make-up was intact. No smears, no dark trails down her cheeks. Her eyes were troubled, but they weren't swimming in unshed tears. Sarah was right about this one. Though he appreciated her natural talent, only now did it dawn on him he admired Shasta's strength even more.

Before she left thirty-five minutes later, he heard her return Sarah's call. He didn't intend to eavesdrop when she told her manager where she'd be for the next several hours, but now that he had an address, an idea began to form in his mind.

♫

The band sounded good, tight as they played. Their new songs were coming along nicely and even though Dee didn't have the strongest voice, she beat the hell out of Bose, who couldn't seem to sing anything without messing up lyrics.

As they shifted to their album tunes, Shasta was transported back to playing on stage, in front of a waving mass of warm bodies. The memories were seductive. She felt the hum of the amps hammering her body, the deep thrum of her bass running through her like electricity. That's when she began to think maybe she could make this work. She didn't have to leave the band. She'd just quit singing lead. Hell, they could hire a singer if Dee didn't want the job. Frankly, she didn't think Dee ought to have it. Her voice was too soft, too sweet, a complete and amusing contradiction to her personality.

Shasta's little smiled faded as she remembered how her lips sometimes brushed the mic as she sang. She tried to ignore how her throat felt—tight, sore, and raw. She pushed through it, refusing to back down and sacrifice their sound. *Their sound.* Somehow, subconsciously, she understood *Velvet Bitches* had a sound. The fans wouldn't allow her to ease up, even if she wanted to, which she didn't. Pride drove her to disregard what she felt happening to her own body.

She thought she could treat it with hot tea. When that didn't work, she tried lozenges. Those were useless too. Oh, how it terrified her to realize she couldn't utter a peep on the bus after the show in Toledo. She'd lied to herself and called it vocal rest, yet deep down she knew something was terribly wrong. When her voice returned the next morning, a little raspy, noticeably hoarse, she immediately dismissed the warning signs and embraced the darker, dirtier tones she managed to get during the next concert.

Everyone thought she sounded great and she floated high on their praise. Bose had shoved the morning edition of the Chicago Sun Times in front of her as they motored their way to St. Louis the next day. The critic's take on their concert was flattering as hell. He even added a compliment to her person–ally, saying she'd never sounded better. Tragically, she believed it herself, purposely dismissing reality in favor of the hype.

She never finished the concert in St. Louis. That's where everything fell apart.

Who am I kidding? Why am I even here?

It was time to tell the band to start looking for her replacement.

Her heart pounded at the thought. The unexpressed devastation left her trembling. Then their agent walked through the far door, unannounced. Shasta's heart skipped a beat and she nearly messed up her fingering.

"Sounds good," Sarah called out to them, smiling with approval.

Dee's arm dropped away from her guitar and she acknowledged their visitor. "What's up?"

Sarah strolled forward, her heels clicking on the bare concrete. "Just checking in. I wanted to see how things are going."

She looked directly at Shasta, probing for answers. Shasta looked away.

Bose stilled her vibrating cymbal and spoke up. "Too bad you weren't here earlier. We've been working on some new tunes. They sound great. Can't wait to hear Shasta belt 'em out there."

Dee swung around on their drummer with a grouchy look on her face. "Hey! I'm not half bad, and you know it. Give me a little credit here."

"You're fine. She's better," Miri piped up, pointing at Shasta.

"Assholes," Dee muttered.

Sarah took another step forward, closing their circle. "Listen, I thought we should get together, start organizing your big comeback."

So that's how it was going to go. Sarah was pushing the issue. Whether she was ready or not, this was Shasta's moment of truth.

To everyone's surprise, the door opened again. They all stared in astonishment as Blake strode in. He gave Sarah a cursory nod then his eyes landed on

Shasta. She swallowed the lump in her throat. Her hand slipped off her guitar and over her racing heart.

He noticed and gave her a subtle, reassuring smile as he walked over. He was the only male in the room, yet he owned it. That's all the masculinity it could hold. Without uttering a word, he came right over to her side and turned to face the group, his support unmistakable.

Holy shit.

Sarah wasn't the only one frowning. "Blake?" she said slowly, uneasily. Her gaze jumped back and forth between them. "What's going on?" It was hard to tell who her question was directed at.

Blake nudged Shasta, settling the matter. "You're up."

She swallowed again and took a shaky breath. "I have something to tell you."

Chapter Nine

The betrayal, anger, disappointment, and shock directed at Shasta crushed her, yet it was entirely understandable.

Dee's pretty face contorted in fury. "You bitch! How long have you been keeping this from us?"

Ashamed of herself, Shasta gave her stunned audience a sorrowful shrug. "I don't know. Honestly. I don't know. Call it denial—whatever. I didn't want to deal with it…so I didn't."

Sarah pinned her anger on Blake. "Why didn't you tell me?"

Shasta took exception to the shift in blame. "Sarah, stop. Blake's been ragging on me to come clean with you guys. It wasn't his responsibility. It was mine, and I blew it. I'm sorry. I just, well—" Letting her guitar strap catch the weight of her guitar she linked her hands behind her head and blew out a heavy breath. "I just didn't want to let you down."

She looked from one face to the next. When she came to Bose, she paused, seeing sympathy and understanding in her eyes.

"I get the voice thing," said Bose. "But are you sure you have to quit? We still need a bassist."

"She's done," Dee broke in, not giving Shasta a chance to answer.

"Hang on!" Miri's back went up and, her hands on her hips, she confronted Dee. "This is a *band* decision. You don't speak for all of us."

Bose glared at their lead guitarist, equally angry at the unilateral decision. "Screw that, Dee. *We* need to talk about this."

Dee's arm slashed toward Shasta. "She burned you—*all of us*. You're telling me you're still willing to work with her?"

Miri and Bose turned to Shasta. Both looked unhappy, but clearly reluctant to vote her out of the group so quickly. All three started talking at once, forcefully, vying to be heard. Then Sarah stepped into the fray, her voice adding to the racket

Blake's hand landed heavily on Shasta's shoulder. The unexpected weight made her list sideways a good two inches. She looked up and they made eye contact.

He cocked his brow at her. "What do you think?"

"I fucked up." She deflated in shame and misery, braced to accept the consequences.

"No question, but what I was asking…ah never mind. I've got this." He removed his hand and, slipping the index and middle fingers between his lips, blew a piercing whistle. The sound was so shrill everyone jumped, including Shasta. Even though she knew it was coming, nothing could have prepared her for the volume.

All five women spun around and stared at him. He held up a peaceable hand and calmly said, "You need to talk. *Talk.*" He enunciated the word to get his point across. "Go easy on Shasta. This wasn't easy for her."

With that, he walked out, towing the eyes of every woman with him. The heavy steel door closed behind him with an audible *whump*.

Four sets of eyes swung back around and landed on Shasta. It sent her back a step and made her even more uncomfortable now that Blake was gone. Not for a million years would she have expected this from him. He'd shown up and stood by her. The guy had her back. *Far-freaking-out.*

What the hell did that mean?

♪

Blake was in his element, his body loose, his fingers practically dancing across the keys as he and his friends jammed. It was all freeform today, each of them coming forward in turn to show off. As Struthers dropped back, his double bass retreating to the background once more, Blake took over, launching into a refrain he'd known by heart since age ten.

Graham looked up from tapping his snare drum and chuckled. "What is that, Bach?"

Blake grinned, shaking his head in perfect time as his fingers rejoined the improvisational thread of the trio. "Vivaldi."

A warm rumbling laugh came from the bassist and he picked up his plucking, taking them in an entirely jazzy direction while Blake and the drummer quietly backed off and let him go.

Blake could feel the music, like a lover's caress. It infused him, brought his bloodstream to the forefront. He nodded in time, carried away on a cloud of abandon.

A sudden knock on the studio window made him turn. Damien was right outside, holding up his case. All three men nodded at his request to join them without breaking rhythm.

"Hell yeah," Damien said, hurrying in and taking his cornet out of the case. He was already warming up his lips before he even slipped the mouthpiece into the horn.

Standing up he took a minute to pick his opening before he raised the instrument and joined in.

The four of them jamming together gave Blake

a euphoric high.

♫

Intending to thank Blake for his support earlier, Shasta returned to his studio and caught him jamming with his friends. The allure of being a fly on the wall in there was so intense she crept into the studio, waiting for someone to eject her. No one said a word. Relieved, she moved to the right and headed into the corner where she could watch yet still be ignored. She slid down the wall to the floor. With her knees bent in front of her, she listened for a good ten minutes, quietly humming along while her foot tapped and her head kept time.

Blake finally glanced over with an easy smile. An inaudible, girly sigh escaped her. She had to admit, he wasn't half bad—for an older guy. Then his eyebrow arched. "Ever sing any jazz?" he asked.

Everyone was watching, waiting for her answer. Already in defense mode, her muscles tensed—her dicey emotions on high alert. She was sick to death of everyone putting her on the damn spot today. "Maybe," she replied warily.

"What do you know?"

Man, Blake ought to know better than to push her right now. His funeral.

"A bit." She stared daggers at him, warning him

off.

His eyebrow rose even higher, along with the corner of his mouth. He was waiting for a proper answer. "Like what?"

Damn him. Relenting, she gave a moody shrug. "I don't know. *They Can't Take That Away From Me?*"

Blake looked pleasantly surprised by her choice and nodded to the others. "How 'bout it guys?"

"Sure, what the hell?" the bassist said. The drummer nodded in agreement.

Damien gave a jerk of his head. "Get up here, kiddo."

She pushed herself up the wall, already counting the beats as her feet moved in time with the musicians. It was hard to forget Frank was the only person who'd ever heard her sing these old standards.

Coming to a stop beside the piano, she raised her chin, defiant to the last, and belted it out. The smoky melody helped uncoil her tight muscles and unclench the knots in her stomach.

All four guys looked surprised and impressed as they nodded along, accompanying her on their instruments. Encouraged, she unleashed her voice, her eyes beginning to glitter with emotion. She couldn't help it, these damn songs always got to her.

She was weeping silently to the soft brush of the snare drum when she reached the last verse and shuddered at the end, her voice dropping to a poignant whisper.

"Mmm," the drummer sighed in a low, soothing hum.

"Very nice," agreed the bassist. "Where've you been hiding this little girl, Blake?"

Blake spun on his bench and chuckled. "Gentlemen, meet Shasta Kovich."

They greeted her, but there was absolutely no recognition there. Awkward. Shasta surreptitiously brushed her eyes and felt even smaller than she had walking in there.

"Ever hear of the group *Velvet Bitches*?" Blake asked them.

Every head swung around to look at her again, more closely this time.

"No shit?" Damien asked.

"Yes." Her admission was feeble, at best.

"How's the throat?" asked the bassist.

"Better. Thank you."

"She's doing great," Blake told them.

The drummer quietly studied her before saying, "That's not where you belong, sugar."

Blake gestured to the drummer. "Shasta, meet Graham Meany. That's Hammond Struthers on bass.

And you know Damien Morris."

"Hi." *Holy crap.* She was way out of her league. These were serious studio musicians.

"Should we try another?" Blake asked the room at large.

"Let's do it," said Damien.

Hammond looked at Shasta. "Name your tune."

God, she didn't know. She just threw out the first song she could think of. "How about *Dream a Little Dream of Me*?"

Blake spun on his bench and began to play while Graham's brushes swept across his set of drums. Hammond bobbed his head for a moment before joining in, his fingers plucking the deep tones out of his tall bass. Nodding along, Damien licked his lips and raised his horn. With a sexy wink at Shasta, he let loose with the first of many sultry notes.

Shasta's eyes fell closed and she was transported by the music to a place where people didn't shrink from their feelings. They expressed them, even celebrated them. How? She couldn't face Blake while she sang of tenderness, longing, and love. Her eyes, coupled with the words, would betray her for sure.

They jammed for another exhilarating thirty minutes before Blake called an end to things. He didn't want to tax Shasta's voice, though he looked pleased with how she'd held up. She couldn't recall ever feeling a high quite like this one. She was practically floating on air. Though no stranger to the heady rush a great crowd can give a performer, this was something entirely different. The way they all sounded together, each in their zone but enhancing the others, gave her chills. She knew she'd just taken part in something close to perfect.

After the other guys left, Blake turned a speculative eye on her. "He was right you know."

"Who was right?"

"Meany. You've been wasting your talent with *Velvet Bitches*."

She strolled over to the piano and casually picked up the sheet music, pretending to read it. In reality, she was shattered. There was no way she could process anything else. The pain of finding herself adrift again was crushing. "Doesn't matter anymore. I'm out."

"You're out? That's it?"

She flipped to the next page, her mouth a tight line for a moment. Composing herself she said, "Out. Done. Dee pushed the issue, Sarah agreed with her. What do I care? It's just business, right? Nothing personal."

The false bravado was for his sake...*and* hers.

Maybe if she pretended, she'd start to believe everything was going to be okay. She could still land on her feet. *Maybe.*

Blake came over to her. She didn't look up. There was no way she could handle his pity too. Getting it from Bose and Miri was bad enough.

He gave her sleeve a little tug. "Come on."

"Where to?" She set the music down and looked at his hand rather than his face.

"Stop asking questions for once and just go with the flow." Hearing his exasperation made her smile.

"Whatever. Not like I have anything else to do now."

Blake locked the studio door from the inside and they left through his apartment so he could retrieve a jacket before heading out.

Their destination turned out to be an old diner around the corner. The cups and saucers had to date back to the opening of the place. They were thick and heavy, the white glazing marred by years of hard use.

"Best coffee anywhere," he'd guaranteed when he ushered her inside and over to a quiet booth near the windows.

He flipped his cup upright on the saucer and looked at her, waiting for her to make a move. "Do you drink coffee?"

"Yes." Shasta slipped out of her leather jacket and turned hers upright just as a server came over with a pot.

The waitress filled their cups. "Sorry, no specials today. Need time to look at the menu?" She was talking to Blake, who was skimming the selections.

He looked over the top of the simple menu and arched a brow at Shasta. "They have great pie."

Pie sounded good, but she preferred salt when she was down. "How are the fries?" she asked, tearing into a sugar packet.

He turned to the waitress. "Bring us a big basket of fries. Mound 'em."

"You got it."

The woman left them and Blake stuck the laminated menu back behind the wire condiment carry-all. "They do a great breakfast too."

"Pretty hard to fuck up breakfast," she mumbled and reached for the creamer on the table. She noticed Blake drank his black.

He chuckled quietly at her comment before turning serious. "Now, what happened after I left?"

She stirred her coffee, staring at the swirling liquid, wishing it would hypnotize, and yes, anesthetize her from the pain and anxiety. No such luck.

Heaving a deep sigh, she said, "What happened? I'm out. Done. Finis. Bose and Miri got argued down. The band is going to start quietly looking for someone to replace me."

"I'm sorry."

"My own damn fault." She set her spoon aside. "It's not like I didn't see it coming." She took a breath and let it out before finally looking at him. The concern she saw in his eyes bowled her over. *Shit*. She did not want to lose her cool in front of him. Swallowing down the lump in her throat, she forced herself to go on. "Thanks…for coming to support me today. It meant a lot to me."

"You're welcome. I know how hard it was for you. So what now?"

"Now? I suppose I look for a real job." She glanced around and her voice broke when she said, "I wonder if this place is hiring."

Blake scowled at her. "You're not done in the music business, Shasta. Not by a long shot."

"Yeah." She didn't believe him. "Anyway, I'm out of your hair now. No more voice lessons. I have one final public appearance to make with the group. After that, I don't know. I suppose there will be some kind of announcement then *Velvet Bitches* will go back on tour without me."

He frowned. "A public appearance?"

"I'm told I have to show up at that Bellamy Music Preservation Benefit thing. And I don't have a fucking dress for it. Formal," she said with a snort of disgust. "Who has a ball gown hanging in their closet? I never even went to prom."

His lips tightened. He was trying not to smile. It didn't work. "Not a dancer?"

She stared blandly back at him. "Only in my apartment."

"I can picture it." He chuckled, set his empty coffee cup down, and looked beyond Shasta with sudden interest.

Forewarned, Shasta shifted her cup aside a second before the waitress appeared with the basket of fries perched on top of two small plates in her left hand. The pot of coffee was in her right. She slid the basket smoothly to the table then set down the dishes and topped off their cups.

"Can I get you anything else?" the woman asked.

Seeing as the ketchup was already on the table, they both declined and she left them again.

Shasta reached for the salt shaker and held it over the basket. "Mind?"

"No. Just don't go crazy."

She gave the hot fries a moderate sprinkle then

squeezed a puddle of ketchup onto her little plate. "Thin crinkle cut fries. My favorite. I love 'em when they're nice and crispy."

Digging into the basket between them, Blake told her, "Don't worry about our sessions ending. I was going to sign off on your voice training anyway. You've come a long way in a matter of weeks. I don't see you damaging your vocal cords again."

"Not likely." It wasn't as if she'd get another opportunity.

He yanked two paper napkins out of the holder and slid one to her then wiped his hands with the other. "I've wanted to ask; do you ever write your own music?"

"Sometimes. Why?"

He picked up his freshened coffee cup. "Just curious. Any particular genre?"

"I don't know." She gave a lazy shrug and dragged another fry through her ketchup. "Singer/songwriter probably?"

Blake quietly studied her over the rim of his steaming cup for an extended beat. The attention made her fidget.

"What?" she finally snapped.

"I hope you'll keep visiting Clara. She enjoys your company and thinks very highly of you."

Shasta felt the painful bands around her chest ease a little at the thought of the old woman. "I will. She's pretty cool."

"Good."

♬

Blake was troubled by Shasta's silence as the fries gradually disappeared. Her pretty face turned flat and expressionless. She looked almost serene, yet she seemed to blink more. It was almost as if she was in a deep REM cycle. There was a lot going on behind those glazed eyes. He could only imagine what she was picturing in her head.

She was so preoccupied, he was half afraid she'd wind up on the wrong train, or get hit by a bus once they were out on the sidewalk again. Alarmed at the thought, he offered to take her home. She brushed off his concern.

"Thanks anyway." She gave him a rocky smile. "I'm fine. I've been looking out for myself for years." Only now did she glance around, suddenly aware this was goodbye. "So—" She rocked back on the heels of her low boots, her body language awkward and self-conscious. "I guess this is it."

"I guess so." He reached out and hitched up her leather coat at the shoulders then fixed the curled collar. His thumb strayed across her slender neck and his breath caught.

She started to blink, rapidly, and shrugged off his hands, masking her misery with feigned annoyance. "Don't touch the leather. How many times do I have to tell you?"

Her sniffle, and the corner of her wobbly smile, broke his heart.

"Once more," he said and grabbed her by the front of her coat and pulled her in, wrapping his arms around her.

Shasta softened against him. She fit perfectly under his chin. It hit him again how her tough girl exterior didn't remotely match the delicacy of her build. She was a woman of startling contrasts.

He closed his eyes and rested his cheek on the top of her head as Shasta gripped him around the waist. The flow of pedestrians broke around them, traffic passed, and the city carried on while they shared a private, grief-stricken moment in the midst of the bustle. He could have gone on holding her, only she eventually sniffled against his jacket, wiped her eyes, and stepped back.

Her eyes were bright, her wet lashes spiked when she blinked up at him. "Stay out of trouble."

He smiled bleakly back and dropped his arms to his sides, his hands uselessly clenched. "Take care of yourself."

She rolled her lips under then covered them with her hand as she sniffled once, gave him a single nod, and turned and walked away. He stood there, watching her leave, wishing he had an excuse to follow, or a reason to ask her to stay.

Chapter Ten

Bose was sitting in front of Shasta's apartment door when she got home. She looked up from the floor with palpable relief and climbed to her feet.

"Where the hell have you been?" Without another word, she gave Shasta a big hug. "I've been worried sick!"

Confused, Shasta hugged Bose back. "I went out for coffee with Blake."

"Why didn't you answer my calls, or the texts? I was flipping out. I was afraid you'd thrown yourself off a bridge or something. Don't leave me hanging like that."

"You called? You texted?" Shasta pulled the phone out of her bag and discovered what happened. "My phone's dead. It needs a charge."

"I'm just glad you're okay." Bose waited while Shasta unlocked and opened her door. "You *are* okay, aren't you?"

Okay was a stretch. She turned the knob and said, "Not great, but better than I was."

They went inside and hung up their jackets.

Bose closed the closet door and gave a little smile. "I gotta tell ya. When Blake Adams came strolling into the warehouse today, you could have

135

stuck a telephone pole into my mouth with room to spare. My jaw literally dropped. It blew me away," she told Shasta. "Maybe he isn't as big an asshole as we thought."

Shasta closed her eyes for a moment, breathing through the painful reminder. She wished she could take it back. "No, he's not."

Her friend didn't know the half of it. Stepping out of Blake's comforting arms today had been one of the hardest things she'd ever done. Shasta didn't know if she was mourning her career, the financial security, separation from her friends, or the loss of *him* more. They were all devastating.

She'd come to rely on him in so many ways. It was *his* voice in her head, helping her focus, correcting her, and yes, encouraging her. His cool criticisms had dropped off the instant she'd shown how serious she was about music. He wanted her commitment. He got it. Once he understood she wasn't there to waste his time, or hers, he'd taken her under his wing and helped her gain heights she'd never reached before.

Like today.

She trembled at how all of their individual talents came together into one stirring and exquisite session. It was thrilling. The exhilaration was an extreme reversal of her mood when she'd arrived.

To look over and meet Blake's gaze, see his approval and pride in her, left Shasta tingling from the inside out. His wasn't the only opinion out there, but somehow, his had become the one she valued most. And she would probably never see him again, outside of all the photos she'd saved from her Google search. Small comfort.

"Shasta? Didn't you hear me?"

She looked at Bose and quietly crumbled inside. "Maybe I'm not okay."

"Oh no. Shit."

Bose rushed over, took Shasta by the elbow, and led her to bed. Once she was tucked in, Bose went to heat a can of chicken noodle soup. She served it with stale saltines. It was the thought that counted.

"So…are you gonna tell me?" Bose asked, taking the empty bowl from Shasta when she was finished. She set it aside then waved her hands at Shasta, urging her to move over. "Clear some space. I want to sit next to you."

Shasta scooted over and smoothed the blanket over her lap as Bose stretched out on top of the covers. They sat with their backs propped against the pillows.

Bose nudged Shasta with her shoulder. "You've had a rough day, but I think I'm missing part of the story. Does it have to do with Adams?"

Shasta nodded and stared at their two sets of feet. Hers were gently swelling lumps beneath the covers. Bose had crossed her ankles, inadvertently showing off her cute leather boots above the blankets.

"Do you *like* him?" The way Bose said *like* was telling. She was alarmed at the thought.

She was going to shudder at what Shasta was about to tell her.

"I think I might love him."

♪

Valerie slammed her glass down on Blake's coffee table and scowled in disbelief. "We barely see each other anymore and this…this vacant stare is what I have to contend with?"

He sank into the sofa with a grimace and squeezed the bridge of his nose. "I'm sorry. I'm not going to be good company right now. Can we postpone dinner and do this another time?"

"I thought I was staying over." Her frosty tone grated on his already strained nerves.

He forced his eyes open and confirmed the ice queen was back, her glare sharp enough to draw blood. "Not tonight. I have a headache."

Her mouth dropped open and she stared,

affronted. "It's bad enough our schedules don't align very often. It's intolerable when they do and you push me away. What's going on, Blake?"

"Nothing. Nothing is going on. I told you, I have a headache." It was true, though he didn't want to be with *her* either. Knowing that was also true didn't make his head feel any better.

"Then take an aspirin," she fired back, undeterred. "I want an explanation. You've been more distant than usual lately." She paused, studying him carefully. "Is there someone else?"

Suspicion simmered just beneath her flawless beauty. Her long ruby fingernails clicked like dangerous talons on the tabletop. He didn't need this now and his head wouldn't thank him if she flew into one of her tempers.

"No."

The denial came so readily, yet once spoken, he realized it was a lie. Before his very eyes, Val's glossy, red hair drew up her shoulders, bared her long neck, and turned warm brown. Her pale ivory skin darkened to a smooth almond tone. Her sharp cheekbones and jaw receded, softened, and her sculpted nose shrank and sprouted a diamond stud in the left nostril. Val's lips seemed to plump and her eyes darkened to a velvety mocha.

Shaken, Blake shot to his feet with a mumbled

excuse. "Aspirin. I need aspirin. Excuse me."

Once in the kitchen, he could barely get the childproof cap off the bottle. He was close to hyperventilating as he filled a glass at the sink.

"For Christ's sake, calm down," he muttered to himself.

His body ignored him. His heart was pounding. He was beginning to sweat under the arms. He was on the verge of an all-out panic attack. His first. A novel experience.

Shasta was just a kid. Twenty-three-year-olds didn't interest him when *he* was that age. Now, at thirty-four, he should find her even less appealing. Too bad the message wasn't getting through. Damn it.

He swallowed the painkillers and set the glass in the sink. Spreading his arms in front of him, he gripped the edge of the counter and hung his head, shaking it back and forth, still trying to deny the truth.

They'd been meeting for an hour every Thursday for the last seven weeks. In that time, they'd had some ups and downs. They didn't simply have an occasional difference of opinion, they had clashes. She'd told him flat out that first day she didn't like him. He didn't care—then. It would bother him now if he still believed it was true.

Fortunately, they not only found they *could* work together, they both seemed to find it stimulating. She'd grown and he'd relaxed. They'd both gained something important in the bargain. The most telling was mutual respect.

Shasta had devoted herself to improving as a musician and performer. She was smart, had a good ear, and a determination to succeed, whatever it took. Her tenacity and spirit impressed him. So when, and *how,* did his admiration and respect transform into affection? *Love.*

Lost in his whirling thoughts, he didn't hear Valerie come into the room. Her touch on the back of his shirt startled the living hell out of him.

"Easy," she said in a surprisingly soothing tone. Not like her at all. "Your headache *must* be bad. You look awful." She began to work on the kinks in his neck.

He allowed his eyes to drop closed, unable to recall Val ever doing something so considerate before. The unexpected gesture didn't change the truth. It came too late to salvage things between them. Their relationship, unconventional though it was, had run its course. He suspected they'd only survived this long because they didn't see each other constantly. The inconvenience of their conflicting schedules turned out to be very convenient. It allowed them to overlook all the reasons they wouldn't work as a couple if they spent more time together.

They led parallel lives and maintained separate addresses. As break-ups went, theirs should go smoothly. It wasn't like he'd be asking for a ring back or for her to move out. But in order to get Val out of his bed and his life, Blake was willing to let her spin the story however it suited her, even if she made him look bad in the process. It was worth it.

Reaching back, he caught her wrist and turned. "Thank you. Let me take you home."

"Don't bother. I called a cab."

After Val left, Blake went into his bedroom for his phone. He picked it up from the dresser and thumbed the number he'd memorized four days ago. The effort was probably pointless. Shasta never picked up, nor had she replied to his messages or texts. When he heard the recording—again—he cut the call and shook his head, perplexed by her avoidance. Damn it.

It was time to put his plan into action, with or without her knowledge. He scrolled for Damien's number and brought the phone to his ear.

"Yeah, it's me. Let's do it."

♫

Val stormed into her apartment, slammed the door, and threw her Louis Vuitton crocodile handbag across the room. It struck the edge of the rosewood table and burst open on impact. She watched the contents take flight. The silver compact spinning through the air before it disappeared behind a chair was mesmerizing. The rest of the items scattered across the floor.

"That asshole! That bastard! I hate him."

Still enraged, and not nearly finished yet, she shook her fist at the far windows, wishing Blake could see this gesture. It was meant for him. *Still* not satisfied, she ripped two of the pillows off the sofa and hurled those next.

A drink. She needed a drink. Muttering under her breath, she stopped by her cabinet bar and grabbed the bottle of wine she'd opened earlier. *Fuck it. Who needs a glass?* She yanked the rubber stopper and took a big, unladylike slug, past the point of caring it had cost $150 dollars.

Blake was never going to commit. Why did she think he would? Their *association* had always been about convenience—nothing more than having a plus-one when the occasion called for it and a safe bed buddy when they were in the mood. She knew it was risky at the start. She'd gambled anyway, fairly confident he'd develop feelings for her in the bargain. Foolish woman.

He'd always stood apart from the social scene she enjoyed so much. He was aloof by nature, which only made him more valuable as a dinner guest and escort. Handsome, intelligent, and sharp-witted, Blake was a man of few words, but those he chose to speak had impact. The less he gave, the more people wanted. Was she any different?

She wandered into her big bathroom and turned on the tap to fill the tub. Maybe she'd just drown herself. Then he'd feel bad for throwing her away. She took another hard, painful swallow of wine and wiped her mouth with the back of her hand, accidentally smearing her lipstick. The sniffle she made at the discovery was involuntary. She was an emotional mess now, and it was his fault.

There was a time Blake had shown her the awesome passion he kept safely leashed inside of him. When he let go, and relaxed his hold on his infernal self-control, he made the earth move for her. The man was night and day, hot and cold, a whisper and a scream. She'd had them all. She'd fallen for them all. He was like the improvisational jazz he liked to play. He made her feel off-kilter, restless, and sexual at the same time. He could lull, or seduce, then shock her with discord without warning before pulling her back from the brink with something comforting and recognizable.

She was a fool to ever think she could have the upper hand with a man like him. She couldn't wrap him around her finger because he was holding all the strings. Had she asked for more from him a year ago, things would have only ended sooner. He'd been phoning in their time together for months, and that was *if* he agreed to a hook-up at all. She couldn't remember the last time he'd initiated contact of any kind. She called him. She left messages. She invited him to bed or asked him to escort her to things. There was a total imbalance of effort. A smart woman would have stopped pursuing it, pursuing *him*. It was too late for that. The more he pulled back from her, the more she pushed and followed up with engagements. Good thing she still had his word he'd take her to the Music Preservation Benefit. It wasn't even something she particularly cared about, but he was interested in the cause. Fortunately, he was good about keeping his promises. She couldn't give up. Not now. She'd invested too much not to see it through. She hadn't lost him entirely yet.

One more slug of wine and she set the bottle down so she could unbutton her dress and slither out of her slip. She sat on the wide tile edge and rolled the stockings down her legs then spun around and dipped her toes in the water.

"Mmm." She slid in, completely immersing herself, and remembered the times Blake had enjoyed the pleasures this tub offered with her.

"It isn't truly over until the fat lady sings," she reminded herself when she came up for air. Of course she'd shoot the bitch before she ever reached the stage.

♫

Shasta dragged the wooden rocker closer to the piano so Clara would be comfortable while watching Shasta's fingering. Her old friend looked too cute for words with her happy smile and soft gray cardigan. Blake's nanny had come to represent the grandmother she'd never had. It made her feel warm and fuzzy inside. Inspired, Shasta decided to give Clara a show and went straight into a rousing rendition of *Here We Go 'Round the Mulberry Bush,* casting cockeyed grins at her gleeful audience of one.

At the close of the song, she turned on the bench and made a seated, yet dramatic bow.

Clara laughed in delight and clapped her hands. "Bravo! Bravo! You've been practicing."

"Yeah." Shasta looked down and away, embarrassed to have more free time now.

"It shows. I think you're ready to graduate to grown-up music now."

Shasta cracked her knuckles and smiled. "Maybe. Can I keep this book? I'm kinda digging the kid stuff—memories and all that."

"It's yours."

"Thanks."

Clara's smile smoothed out and she studied Shasta with apparent concern. "Blake tells me you aren't answering his calls."

"Yeah, well—" Every time she saw his name and number flash on her cell phone her heart gave a despondent stutter. It would be so easy to give in to temptation and pick up. It would be much harder to get over him if she did. "I thought it would be easier just to make a clean break."

"I don't understand."

Unsettled, Shasta looked down at the piano and mindlessly brushed her fingers across the keys. "I'm not his responsibility anymore."

"Oh, Shasta." Clara sighed. "You're more important to him than that."

Clara meant well, but it wasn't helpful. In fact, it hurt to even hope. Shasta crushed the wishful flutter inside of her.

"How could you possibly know that?" she snapped, distressed and depressed as she traced a smooth black key with the pad of her index finger.

"I know because he brought you to me. He's never done that before."

Shasta shot to her feet. Her heart was pounding, her cheeks warm. "I could use a glass of water. Can I get you one?" It was hard to look at Clara, but she forced herself.

The old woman's cornflower blue eyes gazed steadily back at her. "Please."

Things were strained as they sat quietly together, sipping their water and avoiding un–necessary eye contact. Shasta eventually recalled a subject she'd been worrying about recently. Perhaps Clara could suggest something.

She set her glass aside and rubbed her hands up and down the tops of her jeans. "So there's this important benefit thing coming up. It's formal and I have to go. Problem *is* I don't have a dress. Since I don't know where my next paycheck is coming from, I can't exactly chuck money away at a store like Sack's Fifth Avenue for something I'll only wear once."

"Hmm, I see. That is a dilemma." Clara's expression was pensive as she gently rocked in her chair. "Would you consider something second–hand?"

"I don't have a problem with it, as long as it

looks decent. Growing up, secondhand was all I could afford."

Clara came to a complete stop. She gripped the scrolled arms of her chair and leaned forward, eager to impart something. "I have this friend, Susanna. She owns a lovely shop. You wouldn't believe the treasures. Her stock runs toward vintage clothing and stage memorabilia."

"Where is it? Do you think she can help me?"

"I'm almost positive. It's called *Encore*." Clara fell silent. Her brow furrowed, she shook her head. "Oh, this is frustrating. I can't remember the address. I hope she's still in business. It's been a few years since I stopped in."

"Hang on." Shasta pulled her phone out of her pocket and did a quick search. "Just off Manhattan Avenue?"

"That's it! That's the one!" Clara relaxed in relief.

"Thanks. I'll check it out. I had no idea who to ask."

"If you find something, I'd love to hear about it."

Shasta grinned. "If I find anything, I'll take a selfie for you."

Clara laughed. "Even better."

♫

Shasta roped Bose into shopping with her that afternoon. It turned out to be a great stop for both of them. Bose was able to indulge her inner flower child while Shasta moved farther back into the store, looking for something appropriate. As far as formal wear went, it wasn't promising. She hated everything she saw from the bright mint green polyester dress with matching sequins to the psychedelic print in orange, yellow, and red. *Who would ever wear something like that?* She shuddered at so many of the styles from the past, less encouraged by the minute.

An older woman came out from the back and recognized she was struggling.

"Are you looking for something special?" she asked Shasta.

"Uh, yeah. I need a dress. A gown?" She felt like an idiot. There was no way she was going to find anything here. Not based on what she'd seen so far.

"Oh, honey. Those aren't right for you." The old woman pulled the hanger Shasta was holding out of her hand and slid the hideous dress back in place.

Shasta agreed, but she didn't know how the woman could possibly know that unless… "Are you Susanna?"

The woman turned in surprise. "I am. Have we met?"

"No." Shasta smiled. "My friend Clara Hastings sent me here."

"Clara? Oh, my goodness. It's been ages. How is she?"

"She's great. As sweet as ever."

Susanna appeared genuinely happy to hear it. "I'm glad. Now let me take a look at you."

Shasta was confused, but allowed Susanna to pull her into the aisle.

"Could you take off your coat, dear? I want to see your figure."

Shasta set her shoulder bag on the floor next to her and shrugged out of her leather jacket, draping it over the nearest rack. She held out her arms, her eyebrows arched, and braced for the verdict.

"No real bust," murmured Susanna critically, rubbing her chin as she slowly circled. "Long through the torso—that's nice. Oh, you have a lovely fanny, dear. I'm getting an idea. Oh my, yes. Yes, yes, yes!"

Susanna charged into the back and returned two minutes later holding a hanger aloft with a dry cleaner's bag streaming from it.

Shasta didn't know what to expect.

"I just got this in last week. It was part of

Camilla Steiner's estate. You probably don't know who she was. She never made the jump to Hollywood, but she was a very busy stage actress right here. I understand she wore this in a 1953 off-Broadway adaptation of *Dinner at Eight*." Susanna moved Shasta's jacket down the rack and hung the dress so it was facing them. She began to raise the plastic, looking more excited as the gown underneath was carefully exposed. "You have to try this on."

Shasta wanted to. She could hardly keep from reaching for the fabric the moment she saw the exquisite black and silver diaphanous dream. The material looked remarkably fine. When Susanna slid her hand up between the lovely shell and the solid black silk lining, the silver in the pattern shimmered and danced like moving water against the back of her hand. Shasta had never seen anything like it. A dress that exquisite was much too nice for her. No doubt too expensive.

"I'm on a budget," she demurred, even though her eyes drank in the gown, newly exposed to her covetous heart.

"Indulge an old lady. Take this into the dressing room. It's not every day you meet someone with the exact figure for a dress like this." Susanna unhooked the hanger from the rack and held it out to her.

Shasta sensed it was useless to argue. She took the dress from the shopkeeper and was swiftly ushered to the changing rooms. There were three.

She went into the first and closed the curtain behind her then hung the gown on the hook. She tried to look at it critically. Though the style itself seemed fairly plain and rather shapeless on the hanger, there was something about the dress that appealed to her. She couldn't put her finger on it. Only after she stripped to her panties and began to ease the gown off the hanger did she realize the entire back of the dress was simply *gone*. Good thing she didn't need a bra. The three-inch-wide straps of fabric that passed over the front of the shoulders made a graceful reverse curve and met up with the side seam under the arms. The cut was meant to display the entire back. It was dramatic, beautiful. Seeing how low it dipped at the bottom, she wondered if her small tattoo would show. Only one way to find out.

One thing her mother taught her was that a dress was supposed to go on over the head. She shimmied into the gown and eased it down her body, shaking it out as it fell into place. Then she saw herself in the long, narrow mirror. Whoa. It clung in all the right places. The fabric moved like a breeze as she slowly turned to take herself in from all visible angles. It was a shock. She looked *pretty*—even without makeup.

"Is everything all right? Do you need help?" Susanna asked through the curtain.

"No," she answered, still dazed and dazzled by her own reflection. "I've got it."

Bose broke in, "Well, what do you think? Can we see?"

Shasta picked up the front of the gown so she wouldn't tread on it and took a tentative step out of the dressing room.

Bose stared at her, eyes bugged out, mouth open. "Wow."

Susanna beamed in delight. "I knew it! I just knew it." She twirled her finger in the air. "Turn around. Let us see the whole thing."

Biting her lower lip, Shasta made a slow spin.

Bose barked out a startled laugh. "Holy shit! Your ass looks fantastic." Shasta glanced over her shoulder at Bose and her friend nodded, looking dazed. "I'm not kidding. Who needs tits when you've got an ass like that?" she asked Susanna. At the woman's agreeable nod, Bose swung back to Shasta. "Totally serious, Shasta. You look amazing. Love that little train too."

All three studied her as she faced the mirror.

"Flat chests were the height of fashion in the

thirties," Susanna told them. "A lot of the dresses liked to display the back instead. Some women even wore strings of pearls or gold and silver necklaces hanging down their backs rather than the front."

"Can you see my tattoo?" Shasta craned her neck, keeping an eye on them to make sure they told her the truth.

Bose took a closer look. "Just the very top. A tiny little bit of it. No one's gonna notice. Trust me. If they do, they'll assume it's a mole or something." Bose straightened up and told Susanna, "She's got this gorgeous henna inspired tramp stamp. It's small, tasteful. I'm totally jealous."

Shasta faced them with a sinking heart. "I can't afford this." She lived in the real world. There was no way this dress was in her budget.

Susanna frowned, wagging her head back and forth in disagreement. "I think you were meant to have it—the timing, the unusual style of the gown, and it fits you perfectly. You won't even need to have it altered. How much were you prepared to spend?"

Shasta hated to talk money with anyone. She kept her finances close to the vest—always had. It was how she protected herself. So what was a fair price for a dress like this? There wasn't even a tag on the damn thing yet. She'd never haggled in her life. "$250?"

"This is your lucky day," Susanna told her with a big smile.

Bose punched the air. "Yes!"

"*No.*" Shasta didn't want to take advantage of Clara's friend. "I feel like I'd be stealing it at that price."

"Nonsense. I don't give away my stock. I would have lost my business by now if I did. I'm satisfied we're both getting a fair deal."

"If you're sure," she double checked.

"Positive."

Shasta felt lightheaded, elated. She had a dress. "Okay. I'll take it."

Chapter Eleven

A full week had passed since Blake stopped calling. Shasta thought it would be easier without the pressure to pick up, without the guilt at shutting him down. Now that he'd given up, she wanted to call *him*. She stalked him on the computer, hoping to get an updated glimpse of him. No dice. It was as if he'd dropped out of the world too.

On the rare days she felt like venturing out of her apartment, she invariably found herself at Clara's apartment, hungry for news of him, or even just a casual mention of his name. She was sick, sick and pathetic. She hadn't moped this much since she was a lovesick teenager. It was ridiculous. She wasn't a kid anymore. Neither was Blake. She'd fallen for a man this time; a man she couldn't have. Someone she shouldn't even aspire to.

Though Clara had no reason to do it, Shasta hoped she continued to give him progress reports on her. With little else to do these days, Shasta had been practicing the keyboard for hours at a time and getting pretty good at it. She'd never be anywhere close to as good as he was, or even Miri, but she was proud of herself. She'd worked her way through all the music books Clara loaned her. She'd also returned to writing her own songs. There were pages of them—sad, emotional, heartbroken songs. As hard as she tried to jettison the angst and moodiness, there was little point right now. The music was a reflection of her life at this critical moment. She saw herself poised at the top of a dark staircase, afraid to take the next step because she couldn't see where it led. How could she move without knowing the destination? She'd lost her bearings.

So she wandered around her apartment, ate a lot of cold cereal on the couch in front of the television. She slept in, stayed up late, and asked Bose not to tell her how band rehearsals were going with her replacement. It hurt too much to think about it. They were scheduled to leave for D.C. in three weeks and from there, well, she didn't even want to know. She promised to keep up with them while they were on tour. It was an empty promise. More likely, she'd *accidentally* miss Bose and Miri's calls and texts the same way she'd *missed* Blake's. It was going to be harder still to stay off social media where all of their road and concert pictures would be posted.

It bothered her she couldn't be more supportive and happy for them. Though, Bose understood how hard it was for her. Where would she be without Bose?

Speaking of which, where *was* Bose? Shasta

checked the digital clock on the DVD player and scrambled up, gathering the dirty dishes from around the room. She dropped everything into the kitchen sink and was running water on them when there was a knock on the door.

A quick peek through the peephole and she turned the deadbolt and let in her friend. Bose had her hands full. Her left arm was extended straight into the air so she wouldn't drag her dress on the floor. There was a shoe box tucked under her right arm and her purse hung from that shoulder. Her concert makeup bag hung over the other shoulder. At least she was balanced.

"I had to take a taxi," Bose explained on her way through. "There was no way I was hauling all this on the subway."

"No way." Shasta tugged the shoebox out from under Bose's arm and led her to the bedroom.

Shasta's dress was hanging from the hook on the inside of her open closet door. Bose hung her dress from the hook on the back of the bedroom door. She shrugged out of her leather bags and swept her long brown hair back from her face as soon as they landed on the mattress.

"That shit's heavy."

Shasta laughed. "Did you shower?"

"Yep. About an hour ago. Have you?"

"I was just about to jump in."

"Make it quick. We both need the mirror and I hate putting on makeup in a steamy bathroom."

"Bitch much? Don't sweat it. I have an exhaust fan."

Bose flopped backwards on the bed and toed off her shoes. "Sarah said the limo will be here for us by six. Miri and her boyfriend are getting picked up first. Then us. Then we'll swing by Dee's since she's on the way."

Shasta stepped out of her sweats and called through the gap in the open door, "Is Dee bringing a date?"

"Sounds like it. I think it's just you and me going solo."

Great, Shasta thought. She was going to look like an even bigger loser. Out of their band after tonight *and* dateless. The unwanted woman.

♫

Blake lifted the uncorked bottle of wine Val had left out to breathe while she primped. She'd let him in then promptly disappeared.

"Can I pour you a glass?" he called through the open bedroom door.

"Please," she shouted back, her voice bouncing off the tiles in the adjoining en suite. "Could you bring it in to me?"

His head dropped heavily forward and he winced at the thought. *Shit*. He'd successfully avoided her inner sanctum for weeks. Going in there was too close for *his* comfort at this stage of the game. Short on excuses, he knew he had to tough it out one last time. This evening wasn't going to end well. The least he could do was go through the motions so the entire night wasn't ruined before it even started.

"Sure."

With a glass in each hand, he made his way across the cream colored carpet, averting his eyes as he passed the large bed on the left. They'd spent a considerable amount of time on that mattress. The empty moments of his life came hurtling back to him at a fast and furious pace. It was unsettling.

Val was seated at her built-in vanity putting the finishing touches on her makeup before she dressed. She'd had her stylist come in earlier to pull her hair into a fancy up-do. It looked Grecian, or maybe Roman. He liked how her red hair spilled out at the back in long, corkscrew curls. Though she was stunning, Val's beauty no longer moved him.

"Almost done?" he asked, setting her glass of wine in front of the mirror where it was within reach, yet safe from accidental spillage.

"Yes." She dabbed at her lower lip with a small brush, her gaze crawling up his body in the glass, taking him in. "I see you wore the cufflinks. Good. And I approve of the tie. The classic looks nicer than the diamond tip."

He gave his tie a subtle adjustment. His jaded reflection stared stoically back at him. Checking his watch, he told her, "The car will be here in fifteen minutes. You really should hurry."

With that, he left her to it, taking a deep swallow from his glass on his way out of her bedroom.

♫

Shasta applied liberal amounts of mousse to her hair, hoping to control the little wings her bangs had sprouted on either side of her head. Her hair wasn't cooperating. "Maybe I should just slick it back. You know, like one of those femme fatales in silent films? Or better yet, I'll just buzz it right off again. Start over."

Bose stared at her in alarm. "No, don't! I love your hair now that you've grown it out. Don't get me wrong, the Anne Heche meets Halle Berry look was cute, but it made you look a little *too* cute, if you know what I mean."

"Oh god," Shasta groaned. "Cute? Like in,

'*how adorable, let me pinch your cheeks*'?"

Here she'd been shooting for chic.

"Like fourteen-years-old cute."

"Well, that explains why no one asked me out that whole time. They thought I was jail bait," Shasta muttered, giving up on her hair. "Then help me, please? I want to look glamorous and a ponytail isn't gonna cut it tonight."

"I have the perfect clip. You'll look fabulous."

Grabbing her mascara, she studied herself in the mirror as she applied the sable black to her lashes. She'd taken it easy on the makeup for two months now. It felt strange to pull out all the stops— shadow, liner, powder, and blush. She'd even used lip liner. Lip liner! She barely recognized herself. It was like looking at a too perfect face in a magazine.

In all honesty, this night couldn't be over soon enough. For some weird reason, it felt like she was about to attend her own funeral. Dress her up and parade her around one last time before she was sacrificed for profit the next day. Not exactly a virgin sacrifice, but close enough.

Was her dread going to show on the outside? Would people somehow sense she was faking her way through tonight? What would Blake think when *he* saw her? Would she see disappointment in his eyes? Pity? The thought depressed her.

"Hey, you're glaring at yourself and making a pinched line between your eyebrows," warned Bose. She slicked on a deep red lipstick and rubbed her lips together. "What do you think of this color?"

Shasta tried to recall the shade of Bose's dress hanging in her room. "I think it's a good match."

Bose frowned and puckered up to her reflection. She turned her head this way and that and finally nodded. "Good. Me too."

Crap, why was she worrying about what Blake would think anyway? She didn't want to see him. *Much*.

"Oh, guess what, I almost forgot. I brought you the perfect earrings." Bose winked at her.

"Are you serious? I had nothing. Nothing."

"I know. You can thank me later." Bose tossed her lipstick back into her bag and spun away from the sink. "I'll get 'em. They're in my purse."

Shasta plucked at her hair, really hating her decision to grow it out. Volumizing conditioner was right. Oy. Good thing Bose had a plan because *this* wasn't going to work.

Bose breezed back into the bathroom and opened a small box, tipping it toward Shasta. "Aren't these gorgeous? Perfect. You're going to be totally retro. Do I know about this shit, or what?"

"Where'd you get these?" Shasta reached for

them, captivated by their beauty. She carefully lifted one out of the box and held it up to her left ear. The stretched fan shape made her neck look even longer.

"It's only costume jewelry, but you can't even tell all those diamonds aren't real. And the sapphire stones? Beautiful. Gold just wasn't going to work with all that silver in your dress. Did you notice the shape kinda works with the open back of your dress?"

"It does." Shasta put them through her earlobes and turned her head from side to side, admiring them.

"You look amazing. Can't wait to see the whole get-up."

Shasta laughed. "Thanks. Where did you find these?"

"I went back to *Encore* for those skinny leg bellbottoms with the daisies on them. Susanna was holding the earrings for you, hoping one of us would be back."

"Wow. I'm stunned."

Bose smiled at her in the glass. "You're going to turn heads. Just wait 'til Blake gets a look at you."

"Don't even kid about him. If I even *hear* his name, or his voice, I'm going to run in the opposite direction. I can't face him. You know that. Not only did I crash and burn on his watch, but I fell for the guy. Besides, if he does turn up tonight, he won't be there stag. His gorgeous girlfriend is going to be on his arm. I can't deal with that either. I just want to maintain and get through tonight without crazy drama. It'll be easier if I keep my head down and try not to draw any embarrassing attention my way."

Bose snorted. "Good luck with that. You're smokin'."

♪

A gray limousine pulled up to the curb in front of Shasta's building. For the last five minutes, she and Bose had been standing by the mailboxes just inside the entry, snapping pictures of each other while keeping an eye on the street. When they saw the car, they grabbed their wraps and scampered down the front steps, their undersized handbags swinging off their arms.

Bose came to an abrupt stop in front of the driver opening the car door for them.

"Wait! Can I beg a favor first?" she asked him.

"Sure. What do you need?"

"Will you take a picture of us?" She nodded at Shasta.

He shrugged. "No problem."

Shasta passed their wraps through to Miri, who was watching from inside the car. Bose gave her phone to the driver then looked around for the least objectionable backdrop before they stood, arms around each other, and smiled for the photo in their posh gowns.

As soon as Bose got her phone back, they climbed carefully into the car and took the rear-facing seat.

"Let me see. Let me see." Shasta pulled Bose's wrist toward her so they could both look. They squealed over the photo.

"That turned out really good. Send this to me right now so I can share it with Clara," she ordered.

"Done." Bose smiled at it once more then looked up at Miri. "Wanna see?"

"Dumb question. Pass it over. By the way, you two look gorgeous." Miri threw a prompting glance at her boyfriend.

Hint successfully delivered, he finally tore his eyes away from her long enough to notice there were others in the car. "Oh yeah, you both look really nice."

"Aw, shucks, Sam. You're making me blush." Laughing, Bose handed her phone to Miri. "Allow me to say that dress, Miri, oh my god! You look fantastic. I love it. *Love* it."

Miri laughed and smoothed the sleeveless Mandarin dress down her lap. It was black, fitted satin, and embroidered with a stunning dragon and phoenix motif. She'd never looked more elegant. Her ginger-haired boyfriend, Sam, was beyond mesmerized. They were adorable holding hands and gazing at each other.

When the limo stopped for Dee and her date, Bose shifted across to the other seat so the pair could sit together. Dee was stunning in a candy apple red satin sheath dress with a low v-cut neckline and a high slit up the outside of her right thigh. Where Shasta had tried and failed to tame her hair and smooth it back behind her ears for sleek sophistication, Dee had succeeded. She looked like an up-and-coming starlet rather than a lead guitarist. Her date wasn't someone any woman would kick out of bed for eating crackers either. Leave it to Dee to put them all to shame. She put the bitch in *Velvet Bitches*.

Shasta was relieved that everyone kept to superficial compliments for the duration of the ride. She didn't want conversation to swerve to this being her last official hurrah with the group. It would utterly ruin her makeup if she started to cry.

The driver had to make two passes around the Hilton before he was able to pull alongside the curb at the specified door. People were shouting and cameras were flashing as they climbed out of the car.

Someone called to Bose and she brightened and veered over to the throng, kept back from the carpeted entrance by a temporary barrier. Bose tugged Shasta along and they both ended up signing a few autographs and posing in their gowns before giving embarrassed waves and trailing the next batch of arrivals into the hotel.

The hubbub carried indoors and up to the third floor ballroom. The scent of orchids drifted out the open doors along with the hum of hundreds of voices speaking simultaneously. The grandeur of the space and the volume were both intimidating and overwhelming.

"Whoa, system overload," Shasta said a little louder than was probably wise. She'd have to watch it or she could strain her voice in here.

This was where the movers and shakers convened. Those who weren't well-known were well-moneyed, or well-connected. Fame and fortune had never looked so dazzling. Collected as they were, wearing designer labels that cost more than Shasta's accumulated rent for the last three months, was it any wonder she felt out of place? She had a hunch their little rock ensemble was the youngest here, unless Justin Bieber decided to make an appearance. Not exactly his venue either.

Bose didn't look any more comfortable than Shasta. She leaned in and said, "Let's find our table. Then we can go search for Miri and Dee."

"Sounds like a plan." With a sweep of her arm, Shasta gestured for Bose to lead the way.

Once they circled around the milling groups of stylish attendees and farther into the space, Shasta finally noticed the music. Looking across the sea of beautifully set tables, she spotted a raised stage. A pianist in a white evening gown was seated at a black baby grand, providing background music. Most people chose to ignore the waiting tables, but there were a few who'd gone right to their chairs and claimed their spots.

Bose gave her arm a tap and waved at the table on their right. "Sarah said we're at table forty-two. Keep an eye on the numbers, okay?"

It was easier just to nod. There were so many people here, at least two-hundred and still coming through the door. Most were unknown to her, though she did spot a celebrity here or musician there, not to mention a few television personalities.

Someone grabbed Shasta by the shoulder and she leaped in surprise, spinning around to see who'd touched her.

"Damien!"

Even though they'd never embraced before,

they went naturally into an enthusiastic hug.

Then, still holding her by the wrist, he stepped back and took her in, his smile wide and flattering as hell. "Mm, mm. Save me a dance, honey, because you're looking mighty fine."

Shasta laughed. "I can't dance."

He chuckled, spinning her around to take another look at her bare back. "Even better. We'll slow dance nice and close. All you've gotta do is rock back and forth and twirl once in a while."

She could handle that. "Why not?"

Tugging Bose forward, she introduced them. Bose had a wildly out of place fan-girl moment that was beyond hilarious.

"You're Damian Morris? THE Damien Morris? Oh my god!" She stared at his full, trumpeter's lips. "Bet you're a good kisser."

He tipped forward, holding his gut, and laughed his ass off.

Shasta clapped her hand over her mouth and stifled her startled snort. Pulling herself together, she grinned at Damien. "Bose has a habit of saying exactly what she's thinking. I consider it a lesser form of Tourette's, but equally embarrassing."

He didn't look remotely bothered. In fact, Damien was examining the drummer in a very interested way. "How 'bout I let *you* be the judge of

171

that, Bose."

The way he said her name was downright sexy, but when he brought her hand to his lips and kissed it with a roguish twinkle in his eye, Bose was hooked.

Her smile spread from ear to ear. "Maybe I should," she said, daring him to look her up later. Something told Shasta he certainly would.

He winked at Bose. "Until then," he promised then left to locate his own party.

They found their table minutes later and were saved from having to go hunting for their friends when Shasta spotted Sarah on her way over with the other *Bitches* and guests tagging along.

Bose zeroed in on the glass of wine in Sarah's hand. "Where'd you get the booze?"

Sarah gestured behind her. "There's an open bar over there, but the lines are insane. You might want to grab a glass of champagne off one of the trays circulating around. I think they're trying to keep everyone from rushing the poor bartenders en masse.

"Not a fan of Champagne." Bose grimaced. "And I know Shasta won't want alcohol. I might as well get in line. Name your poison," she said, looking at Shasta.

"You're going to bring me something?"

"Sure."

"Cool. Ask 'em if I can have a bottle or can of ginger ale and an empty champagne glass. I gotta pretend to blend."

"You're weird, chick. You're weird." Bose laughed and went to scare up their drinks.

Shasta's gaze traveled around their little party. Dee's dashing date pulled out a chair for her. Miri and Sam were debating where to sit. Sarah put her beaded clutch purse in front of an empty chair and took the seat next to it.

"Darren's coming," she explained and shrugged out of her wrap, leaving it hanging over the back of her chair.

Shasta chose the seat next to Miri and claimed the one on her left for Bose. She knew Bose and Dee wouldn't like sitting any closer. Things were tense between them lately. She was part of the reason. Dee would always act in her own best interests. She wasn't the most loyal person, which really burned Bose because *she* was. It was unlikely Bose would ever forgive Dee for turning on Shasta like she did. There was nothing Bose could say outright against their manager, who also voted Shasta off the island, so by default, Dee got the brunt of the blame on her own. The sad thing was, as much as Shasta appreciated having Bose at her back, she knew it was the smart move. She'd been reckless. They had a sound and wanted her to sing their way—edgy and raw. Ultimately, it would be more destructive to her career than being let go by the *Velvet Bitches* for refusing. Wiser now, she wasn't about to cripple herself to satisfy anyone.

Within minutes, guests began a noticeable migration to their tables. The groups still standing thinned out, making it easier for Shasta and her friends to people watch.

"Hey, check it out!" Miri gave a discreet nod at someone walking between tables. "Isn't that the host of that new show on NBC?"

There were murmurs of agreement, but Shasta didn't weigh in. As the others continued to scan for the beautiful or famous, she had one goal in mind— find Blake. Only by knowing where he was could she hope to avoid him.

An older, distinguished man took the stage and raised his hand to call everyone's attention to him. He eased a microphone out of a nearby stand and stepped forward. The ballroom hushed once people noticed he was about to address them.

Bose finally returned, quietly distracting Shasta from his speech.

"I just saw Hugh *fucking* Jackman back there!" she whispered, scooting onto her seat. She handed

Shasta the empty champagne flute and cold bottle of ginger ale just as the lights dimmed.

Shasta leaned toward her and grinned as she twisted the cap off the bottle. "Did you ask *him* if he's a good kisser?"

Bose snorted softly and gave her a playful nudge with her elbow. "Bitch."

Finally starting to relax, Shasta filled her glass and gave up on spotting Blake, for now. If she couldn't see him, she'd have to trust he wouldn't know where she was either. Not that he'd care, but still, it mattered to her.

A short inspirational film played once the master of ceremonies moved offstage. It highlighted the importance of protecting and preserving old recordings before they were lost forever. It was a beautiful, touching film and would undoubtedly bring in a lot of money for the cause tonight.

When the lights came back up, servers began to bring out the entrees. Weeks had passed since Sarah asked all of them to choose from the menu selections for tonight. Shasta forgot what she'd ordered until an artistically arranged plate of pork tenderloin medallions was set in front of her. It was served with a roasted sweet potato salad and a large, bright green floret of broccoli.

Bose looked back and forth between their

plates, her eyes huge. "Would you consider swapping one of those medallions for a little chicken?"

"Absolutely. You want a little of this brown sauce too?"

"Hell yeah. Put it on there."

A trio of musicians played tasteful background music during the meal. Servers in crisp white shirts and black slacks moved around the tables, refreshing beverages, swapping out baskets of bread, and attending to the diners' needs. Eventually the china and cutlery were collected, elegant desserts served, and more alcohol was poured. Shasta and Bose snuck off to visit the ladies room afterwards. When they returned, yet another group was on stage and there were couples spinning on the parquet dance floor. Attendees were in motion again and Shasta felt exposed and anxious as she hung back, counting on Bose to clear their way through the milling partygoers.

♫

Blake slumped back in his chair, bored stiff, and stabbed the melting amber-hued ice cubes in his glass with the plastic stir straw. The whiskey was long gone thanks to the pompous backstabbers at this table. Expelling a suffering sigh, he looked off and caught a side view glimpse of Shasta moving across the ballroom. The way her eyes darted back and forth made it look like she was expecting a sudden attack from any direction. Her shoulders were hunched and she kept low and close behind her friend. What the hell was she doing?

He straightened in his chair, his curious gaze tracking them. They took a sudden turn toward him and he got a better look at her. What he saw left him awestruck. Shasta was a knock out. The two young women left the wide aisle and walked single file between the tables before stopping at one. When Shasta turned to pull out a chair, he got an eye-popping peek at her back just before she sat down. That was a lot of skin.

He'd had trouble forgetting the Shasta with the black leather jacket and attitude. Seeing her sexy side paraded in public was enough to do an infatuated man some real damage.

He checked his watch and decided it was time to dispatch the troops. Lifting the napkin from his lap, he eased his chair back. Val's head whipped around and she hissed, "Where are you going?"

Where was he going? Was she his keeper now? He wasn't just affronted by her snippy, possessive tone, he was angry. Since when did either of them have the right to ask such a question? It implied far more than they'd *ever* been to each other. The reason things had worked between them this long was because they'd both respected the other's autonomy. Exclusivity and commitment weren't words either raised in private—certainly never in public.

Enough. He'd had enough.

What really irked him was he'd agreed to sit at her table with her shallow friends rather than make an issue of it. It was a minor concession considering he only had to stick around for a short time. She knew he was playing tonight. There were things he had to do. Her *permission* wasn't required.

"Excuse me," he told their prying audience then gently, yet firmly, removed her hand from his arm. He forced a polite smile for her sake, unable to explain why he bothered. She wasn't particularly concerned about sparing anyone else's feelings. Still, he couldn't bring himself to return the favor. Someone else could have the pleasure of delivering that long overdue lesson on reciprocity. "I'll see you later."

As he walked away, he had to wonder why it mattered to her anyway. She was enjoying herself, holding their entire table in the palm of her hand. Val loved the attention. She was right where she belonged. He wasn't. That was apparent. He'd barely spoken ten words over dinner. He was like a masculine bookend—more prop than anything. If she decided to leave with someone else afterwards, he wouldn't object. She'd done it before, though that came to an end once she realized it didn't bother him.

Spotting Damien and the others, he made his way over to their table. They lounged in their tuxedos, enjoying a lively discussion by the looks of things, unconcerned about the formality of the occasion. What a difference between the two tables. One was presently raking their rivals over the coals and sharing blistering critiques of people they'd worked with. The subject under discussion at this table looked far friendlier. This is where he'd rather be.

Blake stopped just behind Hammond and clapped him on the shoulder. "Hey guys."

"Still want to do this?" Meany flashed a perceptive smile.

Blake nodded and smiled at the woman next to his friend. "Cheryl, you look beautiful. Meany doesn't deserve you."

Cheryl gave her husband a good-natured cuff in the arm. "See, Blake knows how to give a compliment without being asked."

Meany slipped his arm around his wife and gave her a squeeze. "I'll make it up to you, sugar."

"I know you will," she said with a confident twinkle in her eye.

Blake looked at Damien. "You're up, Astaire. Watch for the signal."

"You got it." Damien downed the last of his drink and slowly rose from his chair. He took a moment to smooth his sleek lapel, re-button his jacket, and adjust his tie. "You don't have to say it. I know. I make this shit look good." He turned to go then spun back again and pointed at Blake. "How am I supposed to get her warmed up?"

Hammond gave a deep chuckle. "You'll come up with something. Improvise." He gestured to the now vacant chair, inviting Blake to take it.

Damien bestowed his flat, Eddie Murphy stare on Hammond. "Thank you. You've been very helpful."

Amused by the exchange, Blake took a load off and reached for Damien's untouched water.

"Have you seen our girl yet?" Hammond asked.

"Oh yeah," Blake said, coming up for air. "She's going to make a splash in that dress."

"She's going to make a splash with that *voice* of hers. I notice she's keeping a pretty low profile so far tonight. Think she'll forgive us for pulling all these strings?"

"It's a risk I'm willing to take."

They both turned and watched Damien tow Shasta to the dance floor.

Blake didn't want to blink and risk missing anything. His heart sped up and his foot began to tap impatiently under the table. He wished he was the one dancing her around out there right now. What he wouldn't give to hold her again. Too bad she seemed determined to keep away from him. At least she was still comfortable with Damien, though that bothered him more than he cared to admit.

He knew she could pull this off tonight. He just hoped she'd forgive him for what was about to happen.

Chapter Twelve

Shasta laughed as Damien spun her out and back into his arms. Not only did he have moves, he was a total flirt. If she wasn't already hopelessly stuck on Blake, this man's hand on her bare back could have easily messed up her emotional circuitry—big time.

He was too late. Damien never stood a chance.

"You're awfully quiet." He eased back and peered down at her with concern. "Not having a good time?"

She shrugged and dropped her eyes, unwilling to talk about it. "It's all right."

He pulled her in again flush against his body and began to hum near her ear as they swayed. He had a deep, smoky, irresistible voice. She couldn't stop herself from harmonizing along. She closed her eyes and hummed, letting him take the melody. The blending of their voices was so beautiful it sent shivers down her spine.

Damien hugged her tight as the song ended. She squeezed him back, grateful for the dance, but ready to go home. It was time to deliver him to Bose and let their attraction take its natural course. She hoped they'd hit it off.

A few couples left the dance floor. Most remained. She and Damien were the only ones who moved toward the stage. He was leading her in the wrong direction.

She turned and cast a look over her shoulder. "Bose, and my table, are that way."

"I know." He tugged her up a small staircase.

What was he up to? His silence made her jittery. She didn't appreciate surprises. "What's going on?" She tried to take her hand back, but he didn't let go.

They walked out from around the curtain and she came to a dead stop. The musicians who'd just played were leaving the stage and Blake was standing at the piano, too gorgeous for words. Their eyes connected and he gave her a faint smile. God, she'd missed him. It was painful, so painful to see him again. Then she noticed Meany. He bowed to her then took a seat behind the drums. Hammond made a slight nod, ever the cool cat. Though, if his smile was any indication, he looked pleased to see her. He stood tall with his even taller bass violin at the ready.

"I don't understand," she whispered, drawing back in alarm. She looked at Damien, then Blake, in total panic.

Damien gently drew her out on stage and turned

her toward the center microphone. "Sing your heart out, honey. It's time to show the world what you've got."

She looked at each of them and saw confidence, support, and affection staring back at her. Deeply touched, she gave Damien's hand a hard squeeze of thanks. He leaned down and kissed her cheek before moving back, leaving her standing front and center, on her own.

She closed her eyes and focused on her breathing, calming herself at the same time. When she opened them again, there were so many people watching her, waiting. Her heart picked up the tempo all over again. Butterflies battled it out in her stomach. She felt warm under the lights. Fear made her tremble. Then Blake began to play, the pace, the notes, moving her. She glanced over at him. His dark head was bowed over the keys. He must have sensed her because he looked up and gave her a subtle nod of encouragement as the drums, cornet, and bass joined in. Only then did she recognize the song. *Oh god.*

Breathing hard, she gave a nervous swallow and wrapped her hand around the microphone. She leaned in, and with her soft and sultry alto, sang, "More than you know."

♫

Val's hand shot into the air and she threw a sharp look at the woman sitting two chairs away. "Be quiet. I want to hear this."

Ignoring the woman's huffy reaction to her simple request, Val focused on the first sensual chords of a piano drifting over the ballroom. She'd know that loose, seemingly effortless style of jazz anywhere. No one played quite like Blake. Without a word of explanation to her friends, she got up and wandered closer, unable to resist.

Then she heard a voice. It was rich, smoky, and provocatively female. Val felt her blood pressure rise and every muscle in her body tense.

Val cut around and shoved her way through the countless people drifting toward the stage. Those who were still dancing were only swaying back and forth, their faces turned toward the vocalist. Finally, Val managed to get a good look at the woman—and came to an abrupt halt. She wasn't the only one staring. Despite her sexy breathiness, she was young. And far too pretty for Val's comfort.

The singer's head was tilted to one side as she gripped the microphone close. It was easy to see why people were paying such rapt attention. Her emotion was spellbinding, her voice—seductive. Her eyes were closed, as if she was afraid of her audience—closed that is, until she sang the words,

"I love you so." That's when she turned, tellingly, toward the piano. Her captivated audience followed. They all caught something Val had longed for, but never thought she'd see—naked, unmistakable need on Blake's face when he and the girl locked eyes.

He's in love with her.

Val staggered back a step and gasped as her mind rebelled against what she just witnessed. What they *all* just witnessed. Blake and the young singer's very public confession to one another was so shocking to her, she felt faint. How could he *do* this to her? The humiliation! And who the hell is *she*?

Jealousy roared inside Val. Her body shook with it. Her jaw clenched, her hands fisted, she glared daggers at her lover and his presumptuous protégé as they transitioned into *Body and Soul* next. Had she honestly lost Blake to a *kid*? Hell no!

She stood there, seething. Her anger bubbled like lava in a dangerously unstable volcano. She wanted to blow. She wanted to go Mount St. Helen's all over that kid's ass and lay waste to her ambitions. No one, especially not this nobody, was going to knock her aside when she'd worked so damned hard to get Blake to commit to *her*.

♫

The audience exploded with cheers and

applause when Shasta fell silent. Her head dropped forward, arms slack at her side, her chest and abdomen heaving. She had to remind herself to hold onto the heavy microphone because it nearly slipped from her hand. She felt spent, but elated. Singing here, tonight, with these guys, was a rush—the best natural high of her life.

She heard a sharp whistle to her right and looked up to see Blake on his feet, walking out from behind the piano. He was clapping, his hands still in sync with the beat pumping through her veins. His smile was one for a diary. The kind of smile a girl wanted to remember. She broke into a shaky laugh, utterly stunned by the reaction of all these people staring up at them. Then Blake was next to her. He gently eased the microphone out of her hand, slid it back onto the stand, and then he grabbed her in a big hug. She squeezed him back, just as tight, and blinked her teary eyes. The cheers and whistles rose to an ear-splitting level as they soaked up the moment.

When she opened her eyes, Damien, Meany, and Hammond surrounded them. It was obvious they wanted in on the celebration. Blake grinned and moved aside so they could each get a chance to hug her too. After Hammond released her, Blake took Shasta by the hand and turned her to face the audience again. He raised their clasped hands high in the air then, letting go, he eased back, clapping again, his pride in her a tangible thing.

"Shasta Kovich, ladies and gentlemen," Damien said into the mic, his smile brighter than Broadway.

Dabbing her eyes as she smiled in turn at her wonderful allies, she noticed the other group was back from their break. They watched from the wings, waiting to reclaim their places. Shasta felt her heart lift when she realized even they were clapping and smiling at her.

Damien gave the waiting musicians a nod of acknowledgement and grabbed his horn and case. Hammond carefully moved his bass out of their way. Meany led Blake and Shasta off the stage. Just when Shasta thought she couldn't float any higher, Blake put his arm around her as they descended to the dance floor together.

Their enthusiastic audience converged on them, asking about her, and raving about her voice. Shasta heard comparisons to Diana Krall and Norah Jones and wished Frank had lived to see this. She sent out a silent message of love and thanks to him while she was bombarded, and a little overwhelmed, by the attention.

Their prompt to move along came when the performers on stage began to play. Shasta thanked those still in front of her then gladly allowed Blake to lead her away. She couldn't wait to talk to him, thank him. It would be best if it happened somewhere quiet, far from here.

They'd taken two steps off the dance floor when their path was blocked by a stunning redhead with flaring nostrils and murder in her eyes. Shasta's stomach clutched, every hair on her body stood in alarm, and the *fight or flight* instinct kicked her bloodstream into overdrive.

"Blake," said Valerie Walters in a long, ominous rumble. "Who the hell is *that*?" The sharp fingernail she pointed at Shasta looked capable of slicing through her ribcage with ease.

"Val, what is wrong with you? Don't make a scene," Blake warned. Valerie responded with a chilling laugh.

A little freaked or not, Shasta spoke for herself. "Shasta Kovich. We haven't been introduced." With that, she calmly offered her hand, hoping it soothed the woman's overactive imagination.

Valerie's eyes narrowed on her then cut to Blake. "Why is that, I wonder?" She glared pointedly at him.

Shasta didn't care for the insinuation. Not at all.

Blake's jaw clenched and his hand tightened on her lower back. "Not that I owe you an explanation, but Shasta and I have been working together for two months."

"I'm sure that's not all you've been doing. It explains so much." said Val.

People were beginning to stare at them.

Blake looked ready to blow a gasket. "You're out of line, Val. Now apologize to Shasta."

Shasta had never seen him like this. He was trembling with constrained anger. It was intense.

Val scoffed at his demand. "I'm not apologizing to that opportunistic slut."

"Whoa." Shasta's jaw dropped at the unjustified insult. She stepped closer, facing Valerie down. Or *up*. The woman was tall. "Take a chill pill, *bitch*. You're making a huge mistake."

Valerie stepped back, her upper lip curled in contempt. "Don't talk to me! How dare you speak to me? You're a nobody. A liar!"

Shasta never saw the hand that slapped her hard across the face. Her head snapped around and her cheek exploded with heat, the mark of contact searing under the skin. Her left ear rang from the sharp *crack*. The unexpected blow rattled her for a second.

Chaos erupted around them. In the vague moment of processing what just happened, Blake's bellow of fury dimly registered over all the other gasps of outrage and shock. Shasta didn't think, didn't hesitate. Her fist flew before she could stop herself. Valerie's nose crunched under Shasta's knuckles. The woman's chin shot into the air, her heels slipped out from under her, and she landed flat on her back.

♫

Blake stared for a moment, stunned by what just happened. A number of people were bent over Valerie. Two of them helped her sit up and she glared daggers at Shasta.

"Call security! Call the police!" she shouted.

He'd seen this Val. There was no reasoning with her. She was going to distort what happened and play the victim to the hilt. She would ruin Shasta, given half a chance.

Damned if he'd wait around and watch the drama queen work over the witnesses for sympathy, Blake grabbed Shasta's hand and ran for it.

"What about my purse?" she asked.

He heard the anxiety in her voice as he dragged her away from the bedlam.

Without breaking stride, he pulled his phone out of his pocket and passed it to her. One of the elevators was just beginning to close when they reached it. He blocked it with his arm and the door reversed, gliding open again.

"Go, go." He hurried her inside ahead of him.

The door slid closed and Shasta staggered against the wall as the elevator dropped. They both caught their breath.

"Use it to call whoever you came with tonight. Ask them to grab your purse for you."

Shasta nodded and punched in a number. She put his phone to her ear. "Bose? It's me. I need a favor." Shasta plugged her other ear and frowned. "Yes, I did, but she was being a bitch. She slapped *me* first." She rolled her eyes at him and he chuckled in return. "Just shut up for a second. I need you to take my purse home with you." She paused. "Because, we had to get out of there, that's why. Just do this for me." She closed her eyes and exhaled with relief. "Thanks. I'll catch up with you tomorrow. Oh, hey, go find Damien." She broke into a big grin. Her eyes were dancing when she looked up at Blake. He smiled back, guessing what was happening on that end. "He is? Really?" She laughed. "Have fun, bitch. I'll talk to you tomorrow."

Shasta cut the call and handed his phone back to him. Blake slipped it into his pocket just as the doors opened on the lobby.

"Well, this should be interesting," she told him

and strolled out of the elevator as if they had all the time in the world.

He didn't mind following her. That dress was killer, and her wiggle—hypnotic.

They hopped into a waiting cab along the curb and Blake gave the driver his address. Shasta was rubbing her hand and fingers when he sat back in the seat.

"Hurt?" He drew her hand closer so he could take a look.

"A little," she admitted. She let him examine her hand, her knuckles, without complaint.

"I've got ice packs at my place. We'll fix you up." In the meantime, he gently rubbed what he could, hoping it helped.

"How's my face?"

He heard the hesitation in the question and gently turned her chin toward him, using the lights outside the dark cab to see her better. No handprint, no scratches or cuts from Val's alarming fingernails. His gaze softened on her lovely, worried face. "Still beautiful."

She looked taken aback and stared at him, silently processing his answer. He wished he knew what she was thinking. Her reaction gave him pause. Maybe he was way off base. No doubt she thought he was too old for her. He couldn't argue with that.

He agreed.

The tiny diamond stud in her nostril caught the light and he carefully touched it with the tip of his finger. He loved that damn thing. "How's your nose?"

She touched it herself, gingerly. "It's tender, but your girlfriend's is worse." She gave an awkward laugh. "Sorry, but she's a little scary."

He gave a snort of agreement. "I'm sorry about that. She had no right to insult or attack you. It was uncalled for."

"Was it?"

He shifted on the seat to face her. "Let me clarify things for you. First, Val is *not* my girlfriend. She never was. We were friends. It turned into friends with benefits." This sounded bad, even to him, but Shasta was from another generation. She'd probably understand and accept the distinctions better than anyone. "We had a standing date whenever we needed one and no expectations. It was never supposed to get complicated."

"But it did," she said with some delicacy.

Who was this cautious young woman and what happened to the brash and blunt hipster he'd met nine weeks ago?

He wasn't even aware he was still holding Shasta's hand, still stroking it, until she gently tugged it back from him.

"Clearly." He straightened out, dropped his head back on the seat, and ground the heel of his hand into his forehead. "I screwed up. We all have people who aren't a good fit in our lives. You meet them. Things are cool. Eventually, they start relaxing and letting more of themselves out. By then, you're pretty much screwed and resigned to dealing with it. That's how it went with Val. She's a talented actress, not a nice person. Getting to know her was like discovering Mr. Hyde inside Dr. Jekyll."

"Do you think she's in love with you?"

He snorted and let his arm drop heavily beside him. "No. Did you see any tears, any pain back there? It's her ego, not her heart that led to that disgusting performance." He let out a deep sigh. "How do you tell someone you don't want anything to do with them anymore? They're going to ask you why, and you can't tell them, 'Because you're an appalling human being.' You just can't."

"Yeah, I suppose not." Shasta stared forward, out the windshield, her thoughts unclear. "How did you screw up?" she asked without turning.

"I was gentler with her feelings than she is with others'. I didn't do her any favors by gradually easing back from her. She needed to hear the blunt truth. I guess she knows now."

Shasta frowned at him, clearly confused. "She knows? She knows what?"

"How much I care for you. How much I want to kiss you." Christ, it felt good to finally say it.

Her lashes fluttered in surprise, her hands bunched in her lap, but his daring ingénue still managed to ask, "Why don't you?"

He cupped her soft cheek, loving her dark eyes at this moment, those lips, and knew he couldn't. "Because I don't want to take advantage of you."

"Then I'll take advantage of you."

With that, she grabbed his head and moved in, drawing him down. He let her. God forgive him, he let her.

♫

Shasta lost all sense of time and place as she kissed Blake. She'd shamelessly crawled onto his lap. Her right leg dropped off the edge of the seat at the knee and her shoe slipped off, hitting the shadowed floor with a muffled *thump*. She was beyond caring. How could she? Blake's lips were all over her; her face, lips, jaw, neck, ears, and shoulder. His hands were everywhere, searing her skin on contact.

He was still under control after their first,

tentative kiss. She saw the tenderness, his affection when he caressed her face. She smiled back, a little awed by the guy as she toyed with the hair behind his ears. It was hard to say which of them laughed first. Maybe it happened at the same time. One minute they were staring at each other in wonder, smiling like drunken fools. The next, they were on each other like two animals in heat. They threw themselves into it. She felt his big hand on her back, moving over every square inch of bare skin. Then those long fingers of his ventured around her ribcage, but under the dress, and brushed the underside of her breast. *Hell yes!* That's when she went back for tongue. He was kissing her shoulder and she turned his face and crushed her mouth to his.

They were so wrapped up in each other, neither realized they'd reached his building until the cabby stomped on the brakes, harder than necessary, and nearly threw her to the floor. It was a good thing Blake had a good hold on her.

They hastily tidied their clothing. Blake combed his hair back with his fingers then leaned forward and picked up her shoe. He handed it to her when she was done double-checking the backs of her earrings.

"Thank you." She slid it on.

He opened the door next to him and gave her a boost off his lap and out of the car. Her feet hit the pavement as he passed money over the front seat to the driver. Then he was on the sidewalk beside her. The cab pulled away, its taillights growing rapidly smaller with distance.

Blake turned to her, his eyebrows raised in question, his hand out, palm up. "Shall we?"

There was only one answer to that question. She placed her hand in his and nodded. "Yes."

They did nothing more than hold each other on the elevator ride up. He was so proper sometimes. It amused her. But he wasn't as uptight as he used to be, so she'd made some progress with him. She liked to think so anyway.

She sensed his hesitation with her and wanted to shatter it like a chair against a mirror. Aware she was at the point of no return, she pressed against him while he leaned on the interior wall of the elevator. He stroked her bare back, keeping her close, but resisted her subtle invitation to kiss her again. This wouldn't do.

"Blake?"

He caressed her ear, the look in his eyes soft as he gazed down at her. "Shasta?"

"I'm an adult—a *consenting* adult. You're safe. And…I think I'm in love with you."

His cheek twitched, and then he smiled. "You think?"

She went a little weak in the knees as his fingers lightly followed her hairline around her face. He was tracing her the way he'd explored her bare back in the cab. She'd never enjoyed touch quite like this. It was arousing, thrilling.

She gave a soft laugh. "No. I was being gentle with you."

The look in his eyes turned hopeful, hungry. Unfortunately, the elevator opened before he could say anything. They walked out, arm in arm, each lost in their own thoughts. While he unlocked his apartment, her attention strayed to the studio door farther down and she laughed to herself at the memory of Blake sticking his head out and calling her name that first time. Her attraction was instantaneous. Then he spoke, and pissed her off all over again.

Funny how her attraction never waned. Not even when she was angry at him for being arrogant, insulting, and *right*. Damn it, he was right all the fucking time. It took her a little while to realize his initial attitude wasn't personal. Blake was just very passionate about music. He needed to know she was serious—otherwise working together would be a complete waste of his time, *and* hers. She got that now. He cared. He helped her to see how much she truly cared too. Amazing. She owed him for that. She owed him for a lot more than that. But that's not what tonight was about.

"Shasta?"

She turned to find the door open and the interior lights already on. As she walked through ahead of him, his hand strayed to her back, and wound her heartstrings even tighter.

He shut the door and locked it behind him. "Can I pour you a drink?"

"Water would be nice."

"I have wine," he suggested, gesturing toward the built-in bar.

"I'd prefer water. I don't drink."

He went into the kitchen and she leaned against the doorway, watching him get a glass of water for both of them.

She smiled. "Just because *I* don't drink, doesn't mean *you* can't."

"I'm fine." He strolled toward her and held out a cold glass. He'd popped a slice of lime into each one.

She raised her glass to him. "Lime. Nice touch."

He gave her a modest nod, though his sexy, rakish smile was anything but. Their eyes locked as they drank, the tension between them humming like an overheated amp. Then Blake took the final step toward her, cupped the back of her neck, and pulled her to him.

The way he swooped in, and his mouth moved on hers, was beyond intense. Every sweep of his lips shot her body heat higher. He seemed to savor the very act of kissing her, tasting her, and it aroused her beyond her known limits. He'd cranked her to eleven. She needed to touch him, feel him, and lose herself with him. Blake finally eased back, his forehead against hers, and they panted for air. She could feel his heart pounding as fast as hers.

"I want to take you to bed," he whispered.

Her lashes closed at the heady thought and she let out a soft moan. "Please."

One word, barely a hush, really, was all it took to make his steady hands shake.

♫

Blake's bedroom, like his entire apartment, had a timeless elegance and style. The furnishings looked right out of the nineteen-thirties-inspired Humphrey Bogart collection. Dark wood, graceful curves, yet distinctly solid and masculine. She loved it. It suited him.

He drew her to his bed then tipped her chin up, kissing her again. She sank against him, drinking everything about him in, from the taste of his lips to his faded cologne. Simply kissing someone had never left her so intoxicated, so dizzy. She'd experienced lust. This was lust on steroids.

Drawing back from the kiss, he gently turned her and she watched him slowly ease her dress off her shoulders and down her arms. The front of the dress collapsed, baring her from the waist up, though he was in no position to enjoy the full view yet. His hands went to her waist and she felt his thumbs ride up her spine at the small of her back. His long fingers curved forward and lightly brushed over her ribs as if they were ivory keys. He released her and she heard him shrug out of his jacket. It dropped softly to the floor just before he took hold of her hips and kissed her shoulder. When he drifted toward the base of her neck, she dropped her head to the side, offering more. Offer accepted.

Shasta was so lost in what he was doing to her neck, she actually gasped in surprise when his hands moved up to her chest. She opened her eyes and watched with mixed emotions. Her boobs were so small, and his hands so large, she couldn't even give him a decent handful. It was embarrassing.

Glancing back at him, she felt an apology was in order. "Sorry. That's all I've got."

He nipped the top of her shoulder and

whispered, "It's enough."

She decided to live in the moment. If Blake wasn't going to complain, she wasn't going to mention it again. With that, he eased off and his hands returned to her back. She felt the zipper following the curve of her bottom slowly release. The dress collapsed to the floor, circling her overpriced heels.

A gust of excited breath hit her bare skin. "You have a tattoo." He gave a little laugh and traced it with his fingertips.

"Just a little flourish." Not exactly a tramp stamp, but close enough, she supposed.

He sank to his knees, wrapped his arms around her hips, and put his lips to it. She watched, fascinated, and painfully turned-on, as his hands rode along her torso. That's when he found her belly button piercing.

"Oh god," he groaned. "How could I forget?"

He turned her around and smiled at the simple diamond adorning her navel. Leaning in, he kissed it. Then he flicked it with his tongue.

Blake rose to his feet, shaking his head slowly, and smiled like a kid who'd just discovered where his birthday present is hidden. Without warning, he grabbed her head with both hands and kissed her— hard. The next thing she knew, he'd picked her up and laid her on the bed. He stretched out beside her and caressed her naked body. She reached for him, but he caught her wrist and placed her hand back down on the covers.

"Me first. Please."

Though impatient, she relented—for now. He took his time, as if he couldn't get enough of her. His unmistakable approval made her believe she could be beautiful. She'd never been confident about her body, never felt remotely sexy, until she saw herself through his eyes. His naked desire made her crave him even more. How was that possible?

She reached up and tugged at the loose knot at his throat, releasing the tie once and for all. The buttons of his shirt were next. She'd never wanted to strip a man more.

"My turn." She was going to enjoy this. "What do you say we make the earth move?"

♫

Shasta woke to a phone ringing. Not her phone. She felt Blake roll away from her, taking his warmth with him.

"Sorry." He swung his legs off the bed and picked up his tux jacket from the floor, fishing through the pockets until he found his phone. "Damn," he said when he saw the caller.

"Who is it?" Shasta rubbed her sleepy eyes. "And why are they calling so early?"

Blake held up a finger, asking for a minute while he answered. "Yep." There was a pause and he turned back to Shasta with a strange look on his face. "She's here. Hang on." He handed the phone to Shasta. "It's Sarah."

"Sarah?" Shasta scooted up and leaned against the pillows, tugging the sheet over her chest. She spoke into the phone this time. "Sarah? What's up?"

Blake slipped back under the covers and cozied up against her, hugging her thighs. He nuzzled her chest and closed his eyes again. She smiled gently down on him, combing her fingers through his hair. Poor guy, he *should* be tired. He'd been a very busy man last night.

"I've been trying to track you down since nine-thirty this morning," Sarah told her. The woman sounded more hyper than usual. "Have you been online yet?"

Shasta frowned. "Online? No, why? You just woke us up."

Blake pointed to his bedside clock and she saw it was nearly eleven a.m.

Shaking her head in surprise, she heard Sarah say, "You've gone viral."

"I'm sorry, what?"

"The videos of last night. They've gone viral."

Her hand stilled on Blake's hair and he shifted to look up at her with a curious frown. Shasta looked him in the eye as she said, "You've totally lost me, Sarah. Videos? I can't keep up. I haven't had coffee yet."

"At least three separate people filmed you with their phones last night. They got you singing. Two of them caught your little scene with Valerie Walters. The videos were uploaded to the web and they've exploded. The number of hits are through the roof, *and* the *Velvet Bitches* just shot back up in sales. Not just singles, but the entire album. You've become an instant celebrity."

"We have to check the internet when I hang up," she told Blake.

"Okay," he said softly.

"Listen to this," Sarah went on. "I've already had two conference calls this morning. The record company wants to sign you as a solo artist. They want to capitalize on the attention and keep it going."

"Are you serious? Holy shit."

Blake mouthed a silent, "What?"

She waved him off and he chose to amuse himself for the time being by pulling the sheet away from her chest so he could play some more. It was very distracting.

"They're drawing up a contract right now, Shasta. I think you'll like the terms. We need to get you into a recording studio pronto if we're going to take advantage of the buzz you've created."

Shasta grabbed Blake by the hair and tugged him off her breast for a minute. "Do you know anything about contracts?"

"Yes, why?" His interest still divided, he ran his thumb over her tight pink nipple, teasing it.

She rolled her eyes even as she moaned with pleasure. "I'd really like it if you'd sit in on a meeting later. Sarah's got something for me to look over."

He broke into a smile and nodded. "I'd love to. Have her bring it here. Make it one o'clock. That'll give you time to fill me in, and I'll return the favor." He flicked her nipple with his tongue then sucked it into his mouth.

"Um, Sarah?" Her voice shook—her breath shallow. "Bring it by Blake's around one, okay?"

Blake released her breast and crept backwards then dragged her down the mattress by her legs. She laughed, loving how playful he was in bed.

"Hang up, Shasta," he ordered with a promising smile.

She cocked an eyebrow at him. "Sorry, Sarah.

Gotta go."

Shasta disconnected the call, tossed the phone aside, and opened her arms and heart to the man who'd made all this possible—the man she loved.

The End

Books by Tara Mills

Accidents Make the Heart Grow Fonder
Caution: Filling is Hot
Forest Fires
Friends and Lovers
Going Solo
Grading on Curves
In Love and War
Shadows and Doubts

Novellas, Short Stories & Teasers

Britt and the Butler
If You Want Me
Sexual Politics
Falling
Stolen Moments
Holiday Kisses
It's in His Kiss

The Pelican Cay Series

Intimate Strangers – Book One
Tarnished Hero – Book Two
Dark Storms – Book Three
Sweetest Taboo — Book Four

Curious? Read more right here.

Ariela lost everything the day her dad was killed in the line of duty: her father, her home, her school, her friends. Unable to cope without the love of her life, her grief-stricken mom left her too. As a consequence, Ariela grew up wary of the deep passion her parents felt for one another. Since then, she's sabotaged every potential relationship she's had. To her, love means loss and heartache. No thanks.

After years of covering war zones, journalist Dylan Bond is home, though not without scars. Intimately acquainted with violence and sacrifice, he's battle fatigued and desperately needs a peaceful break to restore his faith in humanity.

When an accident literally sweeps Ariela off her feet and into Dylan's arms, there is no turning back. But does she have the courage to love a man destined to return to his risky profession, or will her fear of following in her mother's tragic footsteps become the wedge that drives them apart forever?

How about a sneak peek?

"Please, come in." Ariela grabbed her sweater off the hook on the wall and slipped it on, feeling a little underdressed in her pajamas.

What on earth was he doing here, and how had he found her? Not that she was complaining. Oh no, far from it. He'd made a startling impression on her earlier today. When he'd smiled at her, she could have sworn his brilliant blue eyes were dancing like fairies at a midsummer frolic. Odder still, when he spoke she'd imagined butterflies circling her head. She'd heard tinkling bells. At the time, she hoped it was because of the knock on her head. Now she wasn't so sure. Just looking at him again was doing crazy things to her mental and physical circuitry.

The guy entered the apartment and gaped at the furniture right out of the sixties. Very familiar with this reaction, Ariela laughed.

"Yeah, I get it. The Jetson's meet Beetlejuice, right? Probably not the décor you'd expect two interior designers to have."

He shook his head, still blinking as he took it all in.

Overlapping the edges of her unbuttoned sweater, she hugged herself, painfully aware she wasn't wearing a bra. "Well, there's a simple explanation. When you're cash poor and starting a business with next to nothing, you can't exactly go wild in your own apartment right off the bat. We're still living with the furniture we had during college, courtesy of Uncle Henry and Aunt Rose—with a few freebies thrown in to make it really eclectic."

She gestured to their space-age teal sofa. "Please, have a seat. Appearances aside, it's actually quite comfortable. Can I get you something to drink—juice, tea, coffee maybe?"

Anything, anything at all?

Turning, he flashed a little dimple. "No thanks. I'm fine."

He'd get no argument from her.

They sat down and he looked pained when she settled into the bright tangerine-colored armchair. Understand-able. It did clash jarringly with her pajamas—pastel balloons floating across a soft pink background. The poor guy blinked several times, seemingly trying to handle the color overload. Biting her lip so she didn't break out laughing, Ariela tucked her feet up and gave him a slow, curious smile.

He sat up straight, recognizing his cue. "Right. Sorry. I suppose you're wondering why I'm here."

"It crossed my mind," she admitted.

"I didn't get a chance to give you that business card before they carted you away."

"Oh, and you brought it to me? That's so nice of you. Thanks."

He peered at her intently, more serious now. "How are you?"

Even though she didn't know him, there was something in his expression that made her believe he could be trusted, and more importantly, he wouldn't have asked about her if he didn't honestly want to know. The naked concern radiating out of his deep blue eyes transformed his handsome face into something miles beyond devastating.

"I have a mild concussion." Why was she blushing?

The corner of his mouth curled up a smidgen. "Headache?"

She felt her warm cheeks flare hotter. What was wrong with her? "Not anymore."

"Good." He broke into a full-blown smile and settled back on the sofa, apparently satisfied.

Still reeling from the power of his smile, Ariela shifted uneasily in her chair. "I have a confession— I can't remember your name. It's really bugging me."

His head dropped back and he laughed. "Dylan

Bond."

She brightened. "Like in Bond, Dylan Bond?" She'd remember it now.

His eyebrows flicked up in amusement. "Something like that."

"Dabbles in international intrigue?" She was toying with him, but it was fun.

He flashed a sexy-assed smile. How many kinds did the guy have? "I'm comfortable being in the middle of the action, but I'm back to working domestically again."

Say what? Ariela's eyebrows rose so high she felt her hairline shift. "I think I need a translation. What is it you do?"

He had a great laugh. "I'm a journalist. I just finished a stint in Iraq, but I'm back now. It's nice not having to deal with body armor and helmets."

Looking skeptically back at him, she assumed he was putting her on. "Is that right?"

"Actually, yes." He shifted onto one butt cheek and pulled out his wallet. A second later, he handed her a press pass from a recent event. "I'm working out of my house now—mostly covering the political side of the war."

She read the pass, her doubts dissolving. "You actually live around here?" She handed the card back and he put it away.

"Sure, why not?"

Shrugging, she said, "Well, Lewiston isn't

exactly Washington DC."

"With the internet and a telephone, you can stay connected from pretty much anywhere. Still, I do plenty of traveling and Washington is only a two-hour drive. I can be there and back before Max even notices I'm gone."

"Max?"

His blue eyes were dancing again. Hello tinkling bells. "My retriever."

"Ah yes, I remember him now."

Dylan grinned. "He's probably the reason you woke up wanting a wet wipe."

She laughed and his smile deepened. That dimple of his was growing on her.

"Listen," he said, leaning forward, elbows on his knees. "How about going out with me sometime? We can do something gentle—bumper cars maybe?"

She waited for her retreat mechanism to kick in. It was strangely silent. "Here I was, hoping you'd suggest hang gliding or bungee jumping."

"Anything you want. I'm flexible."

Another perfect smile flashed at her and Ariela's heartbeat spiked. "Sure, why not?"

"Good." He stood and pulled the business card out of his front pocket. "Here, before I forget."

Ariela unfolded her legs and reached for the floor with her bare feet. When she rose he was right there with the card. Taking it, she noticed he was taller than she'd initially thought. She supposed that made sense. How well can you judge anyone's height when you're on your back?

She walked him to the door. Opening it before she could, he turned and asked, "When?"

"When what?" She watched his eyes move as he took an unabashed tour of her face.

"When can I take you out?"

The birds in her stomach were back, fluttering away. Good thing they were keeping the noise down. "Whenever?"

Dylan gave her a meaningful look, full of promise. "Expect a call."

Ariela closed the door behind him and fell against it. If she hadn't locked her knees, she would have been a puddle of melting woman on the floor. As Dylan's footfalls faded out and the back door shut, she pressed a hand to her excited heart. Something told Ariela that she was in for a wild ride with this one. Hell, just sitting in a quiet room with Dylan was exhilarating. Now she knew it wasn't just the concussion. There was far more at play here. Scary.

She was about to find out whether Dylan's hands were capable and steady on the wheel, because he was already in her driver's seat. She knew it, and judging by the look he gave her on the way out, he knew it too. Suddenly the Beatles were singing Drive My Car in her head.

Ariela pulled herself up and wobbled on shaky

legs into the kitchen for a cold drink of water with loads of ice.

In Love and War is available in
digital and paperback on

Amazon, Barnes & Noble, Kobo,
Google Play, and iBooks.

Two couples on a dangerous collision course.

Lauren McKay and Wes Dunlop saw their moment slip away when he left for college. Now, fifteen years later, Detective Dunlop just walked into the domestic violence shelter Lauren runs and the sparks fly, reminding her why she never got over him.

Sylvia Coulter knows if she could go back and give her younger self some hard-earned advice, it's unlikely she'd get through to the misty-eyed romantic. She'd tell her there'll come a day where she'll begin to fear her husband. Sadly, innocence truly was bliss—bliss with an expiration date.

While Lauren and Wes imagine a future together, the Coulter's marriage implodes. Sylvia flees, unwittingly leading the threat to those who offer her sanctuary. The danger at the shelter swiftly escalates, leaving Lauren to fear, is this where *her* newfound happiness is about to end too?

Take a sneak peek.

After lunch, once the dishwasher was humming away and the table and counter were wiped clean, the four friends sat down to a game of Trivial Pursuit. Ken chose to partner with his wife because, he claimed, she had the memory of an elephant. Wes and Lauren were paired by default.

It didn't take long to convince Lauren she'd lucked out.

"That was during Johnson's administration, wasn't it?" Wes asked her.

She stared at him. "How should I know?"

Laughing, he turned back to the other two. "Then we're going with Johnson."

"Unbelievable." Ken groaned. "He's right again. Next time we're playing guys against girls."

"Fine. We'll kick your asses." Sherry boasted with a sneer.

Lauren wasn't so sure about that. There were a lot of things she could say with utter confidence about Wes: he was hot, no question; he was compassionate, he'd proved that on numerous occasions; but smart? The man blew her mind. He was kicking butt without much help from her. Lauren was embarrassed because she didn't know enough to actually contribute anything important. Oh, she'd gotten a few inane answers, not that it mattered. Wes was carrying her deadweight.

"Well, finish us off," Ken said with a sigh after Lauren rolled their pie into the middle of the board. Ken looked at Sherry. "What should we give them for a category?"

Sherry pursed her lips and considered the opposition. "Wes blows at Arts and Literature."

"I do not."

"More than the rest." She grinned.

"Okay. Arts and Literature, it is." Ken drew a card and read it without a word before showing it to his wife.

Sherry's face changed from curiosity to disbelief. "No way. New card," she said, her voice raised in protest.

"Not fair. You have to read the card drawn," Wes argued.

She read it, but with a noticeable trace of testiness. "What British author brought The Hundred Acre Wood to millions of children around the world?"

Wes and Lauren looked at each other with astonishment then burst out laughing. "A.A. Milne!" they shouted in unison.

"I cannot believe they finished us off with that." Sherry tossed the card onto the board.

Wes and Lauren shared a high five. "Poetic justice," he told his sister.

"Yep. We won fair and square," Lauren agreed with him.

Ken was watching his wife, his expression concerned. "Sher, you look tired."

"I'm fine."

"Are those circles under her eyes?" he asked the other two.

"Afraid so." Wes nodded and swept the game pieces unto the Ziploc bag.

Lauren closed the box of cards and gave Sherry an apologetic smile. "You look like you could use a nap."

Just hearing the word nap made Sherry yawn. She gave in. "Hate to break up the party, but fine. Have it your way."

Ken reached out to squeeze her shoulder. "That's my girl." She rolled her eyes at him.

Wes enjoyed a big stretch when he stood up. "I've been here long enough. I'll let you have your house back."

"And I should get going too." Lauren rose as well. "Thanks for having me over. This was fun."

"Let's do it again. Maybe next week, okay?" Sherry worked herself up from her chair.

Lauren brightened at the suggestion. "I'd love to."

They said goodbye to their hosts at the door then Wes and Lauren set off on their own.

She didn't know what to make of it when Wes continued past his own car to hover behind her while she unlocked her own car door.

Then he asked, "What's next on your agenda?"

It was difficult to face him now that she wasn't looking to him for clues. "I'm going home," she said simply.

"But it's early yet. How about coming over to my place?"

Lauren closed her eyes—tight. "Wes."

"Before you shoot me down, hear me out."

She turned and finally looked up and into his eyes. It was a mistake because it was too damn easy to get lost in them, to feel sucked in and drugged by them.

He went on. "I know you aren't exactly comfortable around me right now because of yesterday. Can we talk about it, clear the air? I don't want this hovering between us like a bad stink. Please?"

She exhaled a weary sigh. "I know what you're going to say, Wes. You'll tell me it was an impulse. You don't know what came over you. You'll ask me to forgive you so we can go back to being friends, right? Listen, I understand. You were only responding to my emotional vacuum. I don't hold it against you, so there's nothing to forgive. All better now?"

Wes stared at her, stunned. "*That's* what you're thinking?"

She nodded, too depressed to go on.

"Screw that!"

He spun her around so suddenly Lauren gasped. Then her back was against the car and her feet left the ground. Wes's mouth came down hard on hers. Lauren's fingers bit into the front of his shirt as he bent her backward and his body forced her spine to mold itself to the cool metal while the hot bite of his hips, his solid chest, pressed into her. She couldn't have stopped her helpless moan of surrender if she'd wanted to.

His kiss was bruising, an irritated lesson and her mouth buzzed when he finally eased back and their lips peeled slowly apart.

Huh.

"Maybe I was wrong," she mumbled stupidly, too dazed to see straight.

"You *think*?"

Friends and Lovers

Available on Amazon, Barnes & Noble, Google Play, iBooks, and Kobo.

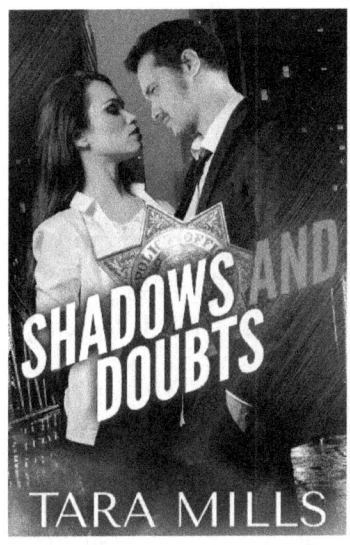

Eden Hennessey, champion of social justice and attorney with the non–profit Civil Rights Watch, just won her biggest case yet—and made a dangerous enemy. Now the anonymous hate mail has turned to threats. Someone is following her, taking photos of her, and proving nothing she's done to guard her privacy and protect herself is enough.

Recently returned to duty after an emotional crash over the death of his former partner, Detective Glen Gold knows he can't afford a single infraction. But when he's assigned the Hennessey case, the challenge of identifying who's behind the threats grows increasingly complicated by their deepening attraction.

As the line between personal and professional begins to blur, Gold's badge isn't all he could lose if he doesn't shut down Eden's stalker in time.

Take a sneak peek.

Hennessey placed her hand on the stack of files. "I had Judy gather up the hate mail from the last six months. I wasn't sure how far back you wanted to go."

"Until we've looked at them, even we can't say," Dare told her.

"I figured as much. Why don't I show you to a conference room where you can read without distractions?"

Following her out, Gold spotted her friend Cameron Bell in the next to the last cubicle, kicked way back in his chair with a phone to his ear. The guy lit up like Carnival at the sight of him and mouthed a soft, "Hi," his hazel eyes scrolling up and down Glen's body with blatant interest. *Shit*.

Hennessey must have seen his jolt of alarm because she was waiting just inside the open door frame wearing a much too pretty smirk of amusement.

"He's harmless, Detective," she assured him as he slipped around her and pulled out the chair across from Dare.

"I'll have Leslie check in with you in a bit. Let her know if you need anything more, okay?"

Hennessey strode over and bent to write a number on the top folder in front of Gold. "This is her extension. Use that phone there for interoffice calls." As Hennessey strolled away, her wiggle as distracting as her perfume, she turned with an interesting smile to add, "The coffee room is two doors down. You can't miss it. Help yourselves."

"Jesus," Dare blew out a breath of admiration as soon as the door closed behind her. "She's got a hell of a strut, doesn't she?"

"Killer legs too." That wasn't all he'd noticed.

———

Cameron came rolling backward into the aisle when Eden left the conference room. His smile was predictable and telling.

"He's not interested," she reminded him with a soft laugh. Cam and his impossible crushes.

"Doesn't mean I wouldn't consider committing a crime for the chance to be frisked by that man. Did you see his hands? He could cover a lot of area with those." Cam quivered at the thought. "Think they'll need to talk to me while they're here?"

She wandered into his cubicle and sank down on the edge of his desk. "I don't know. Maybe."

"One can hope."

"One can." She winked at him.

Cam was right. There was something about Detective Gold. He was compelling, not necessarily handsome. His flaws intrigued her, the thin line of white standing out against the shadow of his jaw. There were two more scars she'd noticed up close, one at the outside corner of his left brow, the other on the same side that scored his upper lip. Details like those merely emphasized his imperfect masculinity. It wouldn't surprise her at all to learn he'd thrown a punch or two. He looked like he could handle himself in a fight, not that he'd go looking for one. No, he didn't strike her as someone who started trouble. The set of his mouth led her to suspect he ended it.

Only today did she get close enough to see his eyes. Limitless eyes, they reminded her of a geode, the crystal depths of intense blue interspersed with shards of gray and green. They were intelligent, serious, tired eyes. He looked exhausted.

Why so tired, detective?

Shadows and Doubts

Available on Amazon, Barnes & Noble, iBooks, Kobo, and Google Play.

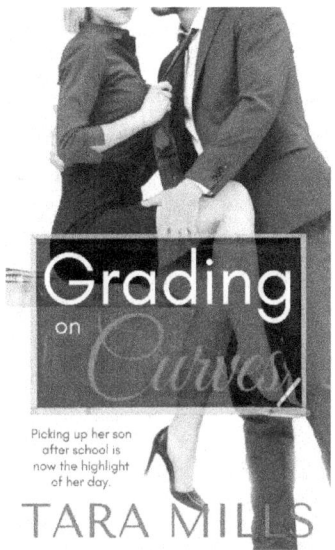

Grading
on Curves

Picking up her son
after school is
now the highlight
of her day.

TARA MILLS

The one time Mia Page undresses a perfect stranger with her eyes and he *busts* her? What are the odds?

Now, this embarrassed mom is running into the hot middle school teacher everywhere. Is there no mercy for the wicked? It's not fair. Nor is it fair her ex is about to remarry, her teen wants his space, and her overactive imagination means batteries are suddenly in short supply since meeting the charming Mr. Walden. He's a twenty-eight-year-old fantasy, not an option.

He looked up, she blushed, and Curt was hooked. It's cute that Mia gets tongue-tied around him. He loves how easy it is to make her laugh, to make her quiver. So why is it so hard to get her to admit there might be something very real going on here between them?

Grading on Curves is a second-chance-at-love contemporary romance. If you enjoy honest characters, funny situations, and sizzling love scenes, don't miss this warm and entertaining story.

Take a chance on a younger man and start reading *Grading on Curves* today!

♡

It was dark and overcast when they stepped outside. Ominous rumbles and intermittent flashes of lightning sliced through the undulating gray clouds overhead.

Curt looked up, expelling a deep breath. "Here comes the rain."

"We could use it. Where's your bike?"

"I walked. I don't live far from here."

"Come on," she said, waving him along. "I'll drive you home."

"You don't have to."

"I know," she said lightly.

He smiled. "Okay."

Somehow, quite naturally, they found themselves drawn together, Curt's arm stretched across Mia's shoulders, her arm around his waist. She hooked her thumb through one of his belt loops and held on. It slowly dawned on her that he'd matched his stride to hers so their tandem stroll down the rows of cars felt right somehow, surprisingly comfortable.

He interrupted her thoughts with a chuckle. "You sure you parked far enough away?"

"I already admitted it was a mistake to park by the theater entrance on a Saturday night."

She hit her key fob and the locks clicked and the interior lights flashed on inside her SUV ahead.

Curt stopped abruptly, halting Mia in the process. "I can't believe I'm considering riding in one of these." He shook his head.

"Get over it. I feel safer in this."

"Three words, Mia. Global. Climate. Change."

"No one said you have to *take* this ride. I'd hate to see you sacrifice your principles."

Curt glanced up at the threatening clouds, the first sprinkles already falling, and sighed. "I'll take the ride."

"You sure?" she asked, needling him for the fun of it.

"I'll get over it. I'm fundamentally unaltered."

"So where are we going?"

"Forty-Seventh and McGowan. You know where that is?"

"The general area. Just let me know when we get close."

"Got it."

They left the mall behind but traffic wasn't any better until they turned off the commercial street. Mia had to pay attention to the road but she could feel it whenever Curt's eyes strayed to her.

He pointed. "It's just up ahead. On the right."

Mia pulled against the curb and put the truck into park.

"Do you want to come in?" His eyes picked up the greenish glow of the dashboard lights and flickered seductively back at her.

The guy didn't make things easy on her. Her heart wanted to answer yes but that's not what her mouth was saying. "I would, Curt, I really would, but I can't. It's too soon." The look she gave him begged for patience. "I'm sorry. I just need more time."

"I understand." Then he grew serious. "I don't think it'll come as a shock that I want to take you to bed, but I'm willing to wait, within reason, for you."

"Within reason?"

His smile was back. "Well, you can't expect me not to try," he said, leaning in to take a kiss. "I'm going to do everything in my power to change your mind. But ultimately, it's up to you. Let me know when you're ready, okay?"

There was a battle going on inside her. She wanted to take him up on his offer *now* but this was such a big step for her. All told, Curt would only be the fourth man to ever see her naked, counting her old obstetrician. Intimacy with another man was suddenly a pretty terrifying thought.

Still, her heart raced like a hummingbird's at the

expectation in his eyes, the confidence that he was going to be her lover. If she was capable of lying to herself she might have felt offended by his presumptions but who was she kidding? She knew the minute she mentally undressed him that she'd be an idiot not to jump at the chance to get close to the real deal. Other women would have tripped her down the stairs for the opportunity he was offering. She'd already met one.

"I'll keep you posted," she said softly.

Curt's smile warmed and he squeezed her thigh, giving her an intoxicating kiss that lingered on her lips after he drew back.

Mia's eyes slowly opened and locked on his. The corner of his mouth twitched and she copied his expression. Curt leaned in again, but this time Mia took his head in her hands and kissed him first, feeling his hands bunch in her hair as they fed from each other one last time. She was sorry when he slipped his hands free and turned to open his door.

"We're still on for tomorrow, right?" Curt asked, looking back as he climbed out.

"Absolutely."

"Good night, Mia."

His glowing smile could have drawn moths if he stood still long enough, but he shut the door and strode across the grass. She put the truck into gear and pulled away, certain she was right to hold off, but miserable just the same. She had no idea how she was going to make it through tomorrow.

Grading on Curves is available in digital and paperback.
Look for it on Amazon, Barnes & Noble, iBooks, Kobo, and Google Play.

Please, if you enjoyed this book…

Read, review, recommend, repeat.

Thank you.

About the Author

I write stories I like to read, with authentic characters and realistic themes. From laugh–out–loud romantic comedy to nail–biting suspense, I've got you covered. Escape with me into books.

In the real world, I'm a happy wife, proud mom, doting nana, and dog owner—again.

Please visit my website
www.taramillsauthor.com

Stories with a heartbeat.

Follow me on Facebook, Twitter, Google +, and Pinterest.